SPIRIT
LOST

Morning
Nell
Bodies and Souls
Three Women at the Water's Edge
Stepping

SPIRIT LOST

NANCY THAYER

Charles Scribner's Sons

NEW YORK

Charles Scribner's Sons
Macmillan Publishing Company
866 Third Avenue, New York, NY 10022
Collier Macmillan Canada, Inc.

This is a work of fiction. Names, characters, places, and incidents either
are the product of the author's imagination or are used fictitiously. Any
resemblance to actual events or persons, living or dead, is entirely coincidental.

Library of Congress Cataloging-in-Publication Data
Thayer, Nancy, 1943–
Spirit lost.
I. Title.
PS3570.H3475S7   1988   813'.54   88-11472
ISBN 0-684-18950-X

10 9 8 7 6 5 4 3 2 1

Printed in the United States of America

FOR CHARLEY

SPIRIT LOST

CHAPTER ONE

G HOSTS AND VAMPIRES WERE KNOCKING AT THE WIDE FRONT
door of the old stone house in Cambridge.

Willy opened the door of her friends' house and looked
out. A chilly gust of late-autumn wind flashed past her into the
house, making her shiver in spite of her cashmere dress.

It was six-thirty, but pitch black already, and here, where
the house was set so far back, behind other houses, the
streetlight did not reach. To get here, the children had to walk a
narrow stretch of driveway and brick sidewalk between two
high brick mansions where ivy flapped darkly and whispered in
the wind. She was surprised that the children would brave these
gloomy depths, even for candy.

Anne and Mark had already turned off the porch lights,
hoping to discourage any more trick-or-treaters. Earlier, the
guests had all rushed into the hall, cocktails in hand, delighted
by the novelty of the Halloween costumes, laughing and
exclaiming and calling out clever things to the children, who
looked back skeptically through their disguises, unimpressed,

3

interested only in the loot. But now the party was established; people gathered in groups around the buffet table or the fire, engaged in their conversations, comfortable, no longer enchanted by the children.

Anne and Mark, who had spent the first hour mixing drinks and passing hors d'oeuvres, were finally settled with the group near the fire. Anne, who was six months pregnant, had just put her feet up on the antique wood box that served as a coffee table when the knocking came. Willy had signaled to her friend that she would get the door.

Now she put the boxes of Crackerjacks Anne had set on the hall table into the opened plastic bags held out by the ghosts and vampires. One ghost had a jacket on under his sheet, but the others were nearly shaking with the cold. Willy started to suggest they go home and get sweaters on. Then she saw a tall figure waiting out in the shadows, a parent accompanying the children, so she only smiled and said, "Happy Halloween," before shutting the door.

"Thank you," the children said politely, but their faces showed signs of disappointment, and it occurred to Willy to wonder as she closed the door if these children had been hoping for something more from this tall dark old house hidden off the street, something more exciting than a nice woman saying nice things. Perhaps she should run around the front of the brick house and jump out at the children from the bushes, shrieking, giving them a good Halloween scare? But no, the parent would probably be furious, and besides, she was cold.

She hurried back to the warmth of the living room and snuggled down on the floor close to the fire across from Anne, next to Elaine Flynn, the receptionist at the Blackstone Group. Elaine was telling a funny story about a lovely but dumb blonde who had modeled for the agency once for a kitchen-floor ad. Willy had heard the story before, and now she only vaguely listened to the conversation that had flowed on in her absence.

She relaxed, letting the voices blur pleasantly into a kind of music that seemed to lilt and leap like the flames that flared and crackled along the log of apple wood.

Anne and Mark's house looked wonderful tonight. It was a vast high-ceilinged shadowy old Victorian, perfectly suited to parties, to Halloween. Anne had decorated it for this occasion with bright bittersweet berries and Indian corn. Fat orange candles gleamed from the jagged grinning mouths of jack-o'-lanterns, throwing shadows that danced with those from the fireplace. Willy had helped Anne carve the pumpkins earlier that day; they had salted and roasted the pumpkin seeds, then munched on them as they worked in the kitchen, preparing the buffet dinner. Later, they set bowls of seeds out for the party. A creamy pumpkin soup sat warming in a silver chafing dish in the dining room, along with a huge bowl of thick, hot chili, corn bread, and a green salad.

How long would it be before she had another night like this, Willy mused, another day like this, leisurely chatting with Anne while they prepared for a party or just a dinner for the four of them, laughing, licking chocolate mousse off the beaters? Willy looked at her friend, then at the fire. Willy and John were moving away. To Nantucket. An island isolated from the mainland by thirty miles of Atlantic Ocean. Where they knew no one, had no friends. Where John would give himself over to his work.

Willy felt Anne's gaze on her, and she turned her head to see her friend's sympathetic smile. Anne knew how Willy felt. Of course they would have other nights like this; Nantucket was not the moon. But the everyday ease of companionship would be gone. Already the intense intimacy of friendship had been broken, by both women: Anne was pregnant and would soon be involved in her family, and Willy would go off with John. Willy did not regret these changes, yet she felt an ache of melancholy pass through her. Like all independent, self-sufficient people, once she let herself become attached to another person, she was devoted, loyal, and unswerving; she would not easily find a friend to replace Anne. But John was her husband, her first loyalty in life, and she would do anything for him.

Now Anne bent forward, leaning over the lap of a man seated next to her on the sofa. "Willy!" she whispered, and made a face, and gestured with a sharp sideways motion of her head, widening her eyes in a silent message.

Willy looked out into the hallway. John was leaning against the door into the dining room, drink in hand, grinning at the young woman who was slithering along the wall next to him, all slinky in a tight black jersey dress. Erica Hart, a young artist at the agency where John worked, had gone slightly punk tonight, her thick black hair slicked up and back and her slim body adorned with lots of clattering jewelry. She looked sensational.

"Oh, Erica!" Willy laughed, whispering back. "Anne, she's lovely, but don't you know she's just a little fool!"

"I don't think so, Willy," Anne said, warning in her voice, but Willy would not be serious. Could not be serious about this, about Erica.

Willy had never been given to easy jealousy in spite of the fact that John was more handsome a man than she was beautiful a woman. Willy went through her life with the kind of innate serenity that came, perhaps, from being an only child who had been adored by interesting, intelligent, loving parents. When those parents had died in a plane crash when she was a teenager, there was the comfort of a gentle godfather-guardian and, later, the inestimable solace of a great deal of money left to her from her family's estate. She missed her parents, but their early love and attentions had taught her to value herself, and so she quite early on became self-sufficient.

And now that she was in her early thirties, she no longer even worried about her looks; she had long ago come to grips with all that. When she was sixteen, she reached her full height, nearly six feet, and she was a big-boned girl, powerful, even Amazonian. This could have caused her a great deal of misery, but her parents and later her guardian had the sense to send her to an all-girl's prep school where she spent her youth quite happily riding her horse, playing tennis, skiing and sailing and charging in a kilt across the hockey field. By the time she started college, she had learned that if she could not ever look cute or even pretty, she could certainly look handsome and elegant and regal, and she hadn't been surprised when men fell in love with her.

She had been surprised when John fell in love with her, but only because she was so amazingly in love with him; they had both been astonished in the way that people are when something seems so absolutely right that it almost implies a pattern in the universe. They had been married for eight years now, a happy marriage that they both lived in as if in a safe and roomy house.

And now there was this move they were making, together, which had caused a renascence of passion and commitment in their marriage.

So she couldn't be bothered with worrying about Erica flirting with John—that would be like an airplane worrying about a gnat. It was more than Willy's natural indolence here; it was, for the moment, a sense of complete security.

~~~~~~

"YOU ARE SO BRAVE," ERICA WAS SAYING TO JOHN. "YOU ARE SO BRAVE I like can't believe it."

John smiled, amused but still slightly flattered. Not by Erica's seductive attempts—she was a gorgeous girl but had been trying to get into bed with John for so long he was almost bored by it—but by her understanding of the courage it was taking to make this move. Erica wasn't as stupid as she could sometimes look or sound; she was only very young. She had joined the ad agency just a year ago and was a quick learner and a good craftsman. Like John, she had wanted to be a serious artist but had to make a living and, like John, found every day she spent at the agency a compromise in life.

When John had asked Willy to marry him, he had not known about her family's money. Strange how the presence of that money had been a burden to him, for if she had been poor, he would not have hesitated to ask her to live in poverty with him, even to work at some boring job to support them, so that he could spend a few years seriously trying to be an artist. He had been told by many people, college professors, art critics, that if he would just keep at it, he had the stuff to be a first-rate artist. But because Willy had all that money, he felt he had to prove that he didn't need to live off that money, his wife's money—it was a cliché that he could not live with at the time. So he had gone to work for the ad agency and had spent years turning out careful drawings that made microwave ovens look like the Holy Grail. In some convoluted way, this made him feel he was showing his love for Willy.

But they had gone past all that now in their marriage and knew how completely they were bound. Suddenly his proud decision had seemed a foolish one—or perhaps it was just that the time was right, now, for him to try to get serious about his work.

He had come home one night in the spring and told Willy he wanted to quit his job, that he wanted to spend a few years at his art. Willy had been completely supportive; more, she had been thrilled. They had spent excited nights sitting up late, talking, brandies in their hands, planning, scheming, dreaming. They had discussed John's desires and needs and how to fulfill them and how Willy could keep happy during the enormous change.

They had been pleased with each other for coming to the

agreement that it was all right to live off Willy's money for a good five years—what else, as Willy said, was money for? John loved Willy for her easy, generous commitment to him; Willy loved John for his ability to agree to use the money, for his lack of any stupid machismo that would have kept him stuck at his job and made them both miserable.

John wanted to move, away from Cambridge and Boston and the ad agency and their friends, away from everyone who knew and judged him in all the slight and oblique ways that people judge. He didn't even want to see the people he knew from passing them on his jogging route, who after so many months would nod hello or ask if he'd been sick, they hadn't seen him jogging lately. He wanted freedom from everyone's opinion and a complete break from the pressured, active, glittery world he had made his own, a world of commerce and hype and pretense and parties and innuendo and slickness. He wanted a major change, a physical move that would symbolize the finality and significance of his decision.

All spring and summer they had made weekend trips to Nantucket, where Willy had vacationed as a child, to Maine, to certain artistic spots in the New England countryside, looking for the perfect place for John to work, a territory and a house that would *feel* right. They settled on Nantucket because it was so far from the mainland, so cut off, literally, by thirty miles of ocean, from the world they knew. They had bought a wonderful old house filled with atmosphere—and they would be moving there this week.

During these past few months, their marriage, which had always been strong, became, once again, after eight years, exciting. Willy and John had gotten comfortable with each other, companions; with the move, they became best friends, conspirators, caught up in a secret that linked them against the world, and they became obsessed with each other, with their plans, their bravery. For months they went through the day as they had when they first met and married, counting the minutes until they were with each other, needing the other as much as they needed air, feeling complete, alive, safe, happy, only when they were together. It was not the sort of mood a marriage could sustain for a long period of time; it was too intense. But it would carry them along a while more, until they were established in their new home.

So pretty Erica, who was rubbing along the wall, closing in on John, wasn't any kind of threat at all to Willy.

Not that she could ever have been. A few years ago, when in the doldrums of his career, making a lot of money for what he knew was mediocre work, painstakingly doing line drawings of refrigerators, John might have been more grateful for Erica's flirtations. Oh, he wouldn't have *done* anything; he didn't want anyone but Willy and, for all the world, would never have done anything to hurt Willy.

But in his heart he knew he might have liked to see how Willy would react, to see if she would have been shaken up a little.

"So like I'm thinking maybe I should leave the agency, too," Erica was saying now, "see if I can, you know, be a serious painter. You know, you really like inspire me."

John looked over Erica's thick black hair, which tonight was combed rooster fashion up and backward, making her look both ridiculous and sensational. He caught Willy looking at him from where she sat curled on the living room floor, her back to the fire. She grinned at John, obviously amused. He grinned back. They were cohorts.

But a few years ago he might have found that grin of Willy's insulting. He certainly would have found it frustrating. If the truth were known, many things about Willy frustrated him; many things that were all part of the same thing: Willy's incredible ease in the world.

He didn't wish his wife ill, but he often did wish that she

had some idea of what it was like to have to struggle for something, to have to fight a bit to get what she wanted. She was so serene. Things came to her so easily. There was all that money she had, and there was her embroidery work.

Willy designed and embroidered tablecloths and matching napkins, bedspreads, curtains, drapes, baby clothes, cotton blouses, negligees, in a variety of styles ranging from floral to art deco, but always vividly colored, with a splendid and unusual mixture that only Willy would think to put together. What she made sold for a fortune in the few select Boston shops, but Willy worked too slowly and painstakingly to make a living from her craft. And she did only what she wanted to do, when she felt like it, for she didn't need to make a living. She didn't need to compromise or skimp or rush; she did only what she wanted, and no two pieces of her work were exactly alike.

The amazing thing to John was that Willy didn't seem to care whether or not her work sold. She was pleased when she got letters or phone calls raving about her work, but she forgot about the praise instantly; that didn't matter. Her pleasures didn't come from outside. It was all interior, all in the work itself. She was satisfied with her work and didn't care if it sold.

So of course it sold. It won high praise. Willy was written up in newspapers, in magazines. And Willy did bother to cut out the articles, intending to put them in a scrapbook, but only this week, when they were packing, John came across them, covered with coffee stains, stuck between some old letters.

Willy's parents were dead before John met her, but he learned from what she told him and from what he could glean from friends of the family that her family had been one of those lucky, eccentric, wealthy, educated, fascinating families that finds everyone outside of the family just a little uninteresting. So there was bred in Willy, John thought, a kind of gentle, unassuming snobbery. Willy was so self-sufficient. So self-satisfied. So content. John never doubted that Willy loved him, and yet he often wished he could break through that serenity of hers somehow; that he could make her look at him not with her clear, peaceful gaze but with the fierce glare of need he felt he often directed at her.

"Well, I think you should think seriously about it before leaving," John said now to Erica. "It's a hard thing to do; it's like stepping off the planet into outer space. But then you're young, Erica. It's been *years* since *I've* really tried to paint. Since I've even thought seriously about what I would like to paint. I've been too busy with other things. Now I'm bound to be rusty. And of course, I'll miss Boston, the action, the agency—"

"Will you really, old boy? Miss all of us, that is? How touching!"

Donald Hood came up behind John just then and wrapped his arm around John's neck. Partly a gesture of affection, this also served to stabilize Donald, who was already pretty well sloshed and found John a convenient hold in a wavering world. Donald was the artistic director at the agency, a likable man even when breathing scotch in one's face.

"Of course I'll miss you, you old lush," John said. Then, realizing just how unsteady Donald was, he turned, aiming himself and his friend toward the dining room. "I'm starving. Let's get something to eat." He looked back at Erica, grinning to excuse his rudeness. She smiled back, understanding. Everyone in the office took care of Donald.

John's entry into the dining room got everyone else headed for the table, and soon the room was crowded with people leaning against the walls, plates in hand. There were almost thirty people at this party, and everyone but Anne and Mark and Willy worked at the advertising agency known in Massachusetts as the Blackstone Group. When Anne said she wanted to give the Constables a going-away party, John had made up his guest list and realized that all his friends—except for Mark, who was a lawyer, and Anne—worked at the agency. And Willy realized that the only friend she really cared about leaving was Anne, and so she didn't bother to invite anyone else, not the managers of the various stores that sold her embroidery work or the various friends scattered around the city whom she had known for years but rarely saw. Besides, she liked the idea of this party being especially for John, a real and symbolic good-bye.

Harrison Adder, the president of the Blackstone Group, came up to Willy as she sat on a wing chair by the living room window, her plate next to her on a side table. She had just taken a bite of buttery corn bread, which crumbled deliciously in her hand and down her front, and Harrison leaned down to give her his usual patronizing, pretentious kiss. Harrison was good at this, at catching people with crumbs on their mouths and bosoms; he loved being elegant and superior. White haired, impeccably dressed, slender, he always made Willy feel like a cow next to a gazelle, and Willy sensed that he enjoyed this—so he was not the true gentleman he seemed.

Willy gulped down her corn bread and wiped her mouth, brushed her bodice with her napkin. "Harrison, hello," she said. "Won't you join me?" She gestured at the companion chair on the other side of the table. "Have you eaten?"

"Yes, yes," Harrison said, pinching up his trousers as he sat so that the crease stayed put. "Very pleasant meal. When do you and John actually leave, dear?"

"The movers come tomorrow, and we'll spend the night here with Anne and Mark," Willy said. "Our boat reservations are for the day after tomorrow."

"Quite a change," Harrison remarked, watching Willy carefully. "Must be quite an ordeal for you."

"Oh, I don't think ordeal is the right word at all!" Willy exclaimed. "This is really an adventure, Harrison. I'm excited! I'm looking forward to it all."

"I'm so glad, dear," Harrison said. "Tell me about your new home. I've been to Nantucket, of course."

Willy was careful as she talked. She was never sure what it

was that Harrison wanted from her. John had told her many times to be wary of him, for like many elegant men he had a bitchy side to him. As president of the Blackstone Group, Harrison was perfect in almost every way: his smooth elegance, his old-money style, won clients over easily. And he was a fine executive, good at finances and at dealing with his employees. But he always seemed to be trying to score points off his best people, John included, in some kind of unspoken game to which only he knew the rules.

"It's a lovely old house," Willy said. "Greek revival style, with steps up from the sidewalk to the front and back doors. Shingled, of course, you know Nantucket and its gray shingles—oh, Harrison, would you excuse me? Anne is clearing the table and setting out dessert, and I really should help her."

"Of course, my dear," Harrison said, rising. "Is there anything I can do to help?"

"You know, you could add a log and stoke up the fire," Willy said. Never capable of telling anyone off, she had become good at smooth escapes. "That would be so nice of you. It's been neglected."

She scurried off into the kitchen, plates and glasses in her hand. At the sink, with running water obscuring their words, Willy said to Anne, "That man! Have you talked to him? He's like Satan, I swear, all polished and silky on the outside but full of malevolence beneath. I don't know how John managed to work with him all these years."

"At least he puts on a pleasant front," Anne said. "You should meet Mark's newest partner in the firm. He's brilliant, everyone says, but so caustic, so aggressive, always ready for a fight. It's just part of the rat race, isn't it, putting up with these people."

Anne and Willy cleared the dining room table of the main course and took their time in the kitchen cleaning up. The two other women at the party, a receptionist and a copywriter from the agency, came into the kitchen with plates, gravitating to where the women were. The four stood around discussing clothes and periods and Anne's pregnancy. Erica did not come in; she always made it a point to stay away from women and kitchen.

"We'd better get the dessert and coffee out on the table," Anne said at last.

The chocolate mousse, trembling on its silver platter, the fresh fruit, arranged in a pretty pattern and sprinkled very lightly with powdered sugar, and the silver pots of coffee and decaffeinated coffee were set out on the long dining room table. Once again the party moved back into the dining room, and conversation slowed as everyone ate. Willy and Anne moved around the two front rooms, setting out trays with liqueur glasses and a selection of after-dinner drinks that glistened like liquid emeralds, rubies, and topaz in their bottles. The fire blazed in the living room, throwing off dancing lights, and Anne and Willy stood together a moment, smiling at each other, appreciating the splendid moment. Laughter came from the dining room, and then the sound of conversation picked up, and people began drifting into the living room, jovial now, replete.

"This is a lovely party, Anne," Willy said.

Anne looked at Willy, and her smile faded. "Something's going to happen tonight, Willy," she said.

"What?" Willy asked, startled.

"Nothing *bad*—I don't think," Anne said. One of her guests was approaching her with open arms, wanting to give her a big hug of thanks for the delicious meal. Anne looked back at Willy. "Just be prepared," she said. "I think it's okay." And then, to the man who was hugging her, "Oh, Scott, I'm so glad you enjoyed it."

Willy moved around the room slowly, puzzled. John came up behind her and put his arms around her. Willy was a tall

15

woman, and John, short for a man, could just nestle his chin into her shoulder.

"Having a good time?" he asked.

"Lovely," Willy said. "John—" she began, wanting to tell him what Anne had said, but she was interrupted.

All the lights in the house went out at once. It was as shocking as being slapped with cold water. The receptionist shrieked once, and one man rumbled, "What's going on!" It was a few seconds before everyone's eyes could adjust to the dim and flickering light thrown off from the fireplace and jack-o'-lanterns.

Harrison Adder's distinct voice rang out: "Looks like you've lost your electricity, Mark. Where's your fuse box?"

Mark said, "In the basement. John, come help me, will you?"

John suspected a setup immediately, since his friend was clear across the room. But he cheerfully left his wife's side and went out to the hall with Mark, intending to follow him down the hall to the door to the basement.

Instead, he stopped in his tracks, startled, for an instant half-afraid. Coming down the dark hall toward him was a glowing ghostly head that bobbed a good ten feet above the floor, nearly hitting the ceiling of the old Victorian house. The air was filled with strange creaking, whirring sounds interrupted now and then by low, malicious, gleeful laughter. The thing that approached him had glowing green eyes and a glowing, wavering green mouth.

The party had come to the wide double doorway that led into the hall, and now someone from that group screamed.

"Jesus!" Donald Hood shouted. "What the fuck's that thing?"

A high, spooky "whoooooo" filled the air. Here and there in the party nervous laughs broke out. The firelight from the living room could not illuminate the dark hall, and while everyone knew this had to be a trick, the effect was still eerie.

"Whoooooo," the thing said again, its voice mournful. Then, "John Constable," it said, drawing each syllable out like a howl. "John Con-sta-ble—"

The tall glowing thing had halted by the door under the staircase at the back of the hall. It was far enough away that John could not yet make out exactly what it was. He knew it was a joke of some kind, but he was uneasy, unsure what was expected of him.

"John Constable, I want you," the thing said.

"John," Willy said, and pushed through to his side. She put her hand on his arm.

Always a good sport, John laughed, although there was more than a little of the boy whistling in the dark in his bravery. "I'm John Constable," he said. "What do you want?"

"Follow me," the ghostlike creature said, and turned.

John could just make out, through the darkness, the wavering dark length with the glowing head retreating down the hallway. Nervously, John followed. It helped to know that Willy was right behind him, and right behind her, he sensed the rest of the party coming along. Everyone was so quiet; that scared him, too. There was no laughter; there were no catcalls or dares yelled out. Just the rustling noises of so many people coming behind him in the dark.

The ghost, or whatever it was, turned the corner, disappearing through a door into what John knew to be Mark's study.

Everything had been changed here. Mark's desk had been pushed into a corner, and the large oak-paneled room was filled now with folding chairs. Tall candles sitting on the fireplace mantle and the windowsills illuminated the room enough so that John could see a large projection screen set up at one end of the room.

The creature had retreated behind a high Chinese folding screen in a back corner. Its eerie glowing head bobbed just above the screen.

"Take a seat, everyone," the thing said, its voice deep and

commanding now. "Especially you, John Constable. Take a seat in the front."

It was odd to be in this room, which was as familiar to John as his own study at home, odd to be in it when it was so strangely arranged. But John took a seat at the front of the room, and Willy sat next to him, once again putting her hand on his arm. Strange noises—creaks and groans and mad laughter and whispers—filled the room, obscuring the noise the other guests made as they cautiously filed in and took seats in the folding chairs. It was odd how pervasive the ghostly noises were, as if they came from the house itself, as if this large, old, powerful secret-filled house had found its voice.

"Do you know what this is, John?" Willy asked in a whisper. They both could hear people around them asking each other similar questions.

"No," John said. "Some kind of joke, I'm sure."

"It's creepy," Willy said.

John put his arm around Willy and pulled her to him. "Don't worry," he said. "It's just some kind of foolish trick. This is a party, remember?" He tried for lightness in his voice, but it came with difficulty in this dark room where the candlelight flickered and the glowing ghostly head bobbed and waved, its eyes and mouth now flashing, now dimming, now gleaming.

"Is everyone comfortable?" the creature asked in its sonorous voice. "Are *you* comfortable, John Constable?"

"I'm comfortable," John replied, going along with it all.

"Then I will present you with your own special show," the ghost said. "John Constable—behold your life!"

A familiar mechanical noise began; a gentle hum. John turned and saw Harrison Adder at the back of the room, bent over a slide projector. Ominous music filled the air, organ music in a minor key.

The screen at the front of the room filled. In great crooked dripping black letters on a red background the words read:

JOHN CONSTABLE: THE GHOSTS OF HALLOWEEN!

The slide projector clicked, and the music changed to sweet notes from a violin, perhaps Vivaldi. The screen now read:

THE GHOST OF HALLOWEEN PAST
JOHN CONSTABLE COMES TO THE BLACKSTONE GROUP

There was a click, and then a picture flashed on the screen, bright with colors, fitting perfectly with the pleasant music. It was a shot taken when John had first joined the Blackstone Group; in fact, it had been used by the agency as promotional material for their group. The center of the picture showed John seated at a high worktable, pen in hand, sketching out a model kitchen. A long-haired pretty young woman artist leaned over one side of the drawing board, her pencil pointing at the top of John's sketch, and Harrison Adder and Donald Hood leaned in from the other side. Harrison's hand was on John's shoulder. It was the perfect picture of friendly artistic collaboration.

"Yay!" Donald Hood yelled, and began clapping. His drunken hearty shout broke the tension in the room, and everyone else began to clap and shout out hoorays.

The projector clicked: more dripping black letters against red.

THE GHOST OF HALLOWEEN PRESENT
JOHN CONSTABLE REMAINS AT THE BLACKSTONE GROUP

The music changed now to a swift-moving upbeat rock song. The slide projector clicked, and on the screen was another shot of John, this one taken quite recently, without his realizing it. Looking at it, John thought he knew who had done it and when: Erica, when she was messing around in the office one day with a camera, mugging it up, saying it had no film, pretending to be a fashion photographer.

19

In this shot John was wearing a striped button-down shirt with the sleeves rolled up. He was leaning back at his desk, relaxed and smiling, talking to Donald Hood and two other men, accountants with the firm. His dark brown hair was mussed slightly, falling down over his forehead, making him look younger than his thirty years, and he radiated good health, good looks, and happiness.

John grinned to see himself. It pleased him to see himself looking so handsome.

"Aren't you something!" Willy whispered to him, squeezing his arm.

The clapping and shouting and cheering continued in the rest of the room. "All *right,* John!" someone shouted.

The slide projector clicked.

THE GHOST OF HALLOWEEN FUTURE
JOHN CONSTABLE LEAVES THE BLACKSTONE GROUP

The music changed drastically now, to funereal tones of dark organ and slow drums, storm music, orphan music, death music.

A picture flashed on the screen. There stood a man who looked like John, with the same dark hair falling over his forehead. This John Constable was slouching on a sidewalk, dressed like a bum, wearing clothes ragged and torn and three sizes too big for him. His dark hair had gone gray; it was shaggy and dirty, hanging in unkempt lumps around his head. His face was white except for the black circles around his eyes, and his posture had changed; he was shrunken, stooped, and bent. Next to him on the sidewalk was a sign: Portraits and Landscapes One Dollar. Around his feet and leaning against the brick wall were several paintings and sketches, all tattered at the edges, all amateurishly done, stick figures, flat perspectives, jarring colors. There was a hat on the sidewalk with coins in it. It was a portrait of an artist in ludicrous defeat.

John felt as if someone had just kicked him in the stomach. Willy clutched his arm. "John!" she said. The room went silent around them.

"Shit, man," Mark exclaimed from somewhere behind them in the dark.

A sick sinking feeling filled John, as if a fortune-teller had just prophesied his ruin.

He felt cursed by this picture, this vision of him as an artist on his own. He wanted to rise and smash his fist through the screen.

But before he could do so, the slide projector clicked.

White letters on the black screen read:

GHOST OF HALLOWEEN FUTURE, VERSION NUMBER TWO JOHN CONSTABLE RETURNS TO THE BLACKSTONE GROUP

Once again was flashed on the picture of John happily relaxing in his office, looking healthy and pleased with himself. The music changed back to a bouncy rock-and-roll song. A few people in the room began to cheer and clap. The music picked up in beat and volume, and the screen changed again.

WE'LL MISS YOU, JOHN!
COME BACK ANYTIME!
BEST WISHES FROM THE BLACKSTONE GROUP

Now the room was filled with cheering and clapping. The screen went blank, the lights came on, and people rose, some still clapping. A sense of relief rushed through the air, as obvious as a perfume.

"Harrison did this, the bastard," John said through clenched teeth to Willy. "I'd like to knock his face in."

Willy grabbed John's arm, held it tight. "Johnny," she said, keeping her voice low. "No. He meant well. It was stupid, I know, but I'm sure he just wanted to show you how much he hates to lose you."

"Did you know about this?" John asked Willy, glaring at her.

"No, John, I promise," Willy said. She was surprised at the intensity of his anger. "Johnny, don't be so upset. It wasn't meant unkindly, I'm sure."

"It's like a fucking *curse*, Willy, surely you can see that!" John said. "I'm going to tell him off."

He half rose from his chair, but Willy pulled him back down beside her. "No, John, now calm down," she said. "You're taking this the wrong way."

"Damn it, Willy, why do you always want to hide from confrontations, why do you always have to back away from things?" John asked, directing his anger at his wife.

But there was no time for Willy to respond, because now Harrison Adder was walking to the front of the room. At the same time, the ghostly head was coming out from behind the Chinese screen in the corner. Now that the lights were on, everyone could see that the creature was really a man on stilts with a long black sheet covering him from shoulders to ankles. The head was made of light white plastic, the eyes and mouth trimmed out with phosphorescent paint.

"DA-DA!" the creature said, and simultaneously lifted off his head and whisked off the black robes to reveal the stilts. He jumped down, a young man in jeans and a sweatshirt, a young man who looked, with his dark hair and eyes and his handsomeness, very much like John Constable.

Harrison Adder began to applaud the actor, and the rest of the room took it up, joined in the applause.

"May I present Mike Upton, thespian and spook," Harrison said, and the young man bowed. People clapped.

"John, will you join us a moment?" Harrison asked, smiling.

Willy felt John's angry intentions and gently pressed his arm. John rose and took the few steps from his chair to the spot just in front of the screen where his former boss and the actor stood.

"Amazing resemblance, don't you think?" Harrison said, and people called out agreement.

John shook hands with the actor, who had only been performing his job. Struggling between his instinctive need to bash Harrison in the face and his knowledge of Willy's gentle dissuasion, John managed neither a smile nor a frown. He looked uncomfortable, and unhappy.

Now Harrison was talking to John, telling him how much they would all miss him, how he was always welcome back, and how they all wished him well in his artistic endeavors, in spite of their little jibe tonight. As proof of their good wishes, Harrison walked over behind Mark's desk and came back to hand John a large present wrapped in silver paper. It turned out to be a sumptuous leather portfolio.

John took a deep breath of surprise. He should have remembered how good Harrison was at this sort of thing, at praising you, then hammering you with criticism, or, conversely, at calling you on the carpet and haranguing you till you were sick to your stomach, then tossing a gift your way, a new account, a carpet for your office, something lavish, so that you couldn't be angry but instead felt as weak and confused as a child.

"Thank you," John said, for what else could he say? "I'll miss you all, too," he went on, knowing that this was required of him but also beginning to feel it as he stared out into the room where the people he had worked with for the last eight years were gathered. He saw Donald Hood, who now leaned drunkenly against the wall, and knew that Donald drunk was better than most people at their sober best. He saw Bob Dedmond, with whom he played tennis on weekends, and Roger Strout, who had worked with him on all the major advertising campaigns; they usually had a drink together after work. He saw Erica, who was beautiful and who loved him unrequitedly; and it was always nice to be loved. With the exception of Harrison Adder, he felt affection for everyone in this room, and he knew he would miss them greatly—they had become his world.

"Well," John said, "I'm not good at speeches. I guess that's why I draw. I'm better with pictures than words. But I don't think I could draw what I'm feeling now or what I'm seeing. If I did try to put it in words, I guess it would have to be some kind of metaphor, a corny metaphor, too, like a picture of a fine and unique jigsaw puzzle, where all the pieces were beautiful, and fit, or maybe a drawing of an elegant and elite social club where only the best belong. I'm sorry to be leaving you all, and I have to say that I hope the future holds a better prospect for me than the one you've prophesied, but no matter what, I think you all know I'll remember you all with great affection, and in a way, I'll always stay a part of you. Of the Blackstone Group. Oh—and thanks again for this," he added, holding the portfolio high.

There was applause. Erica was crying openly. Willy was looking pleased, her smile on him as warm as the sun. The sound of corks popping shot through the air, and John saw, at the back of the room, Donald opening champagne and pouring it into tall crystal glasses as Mark entered the room with more bottles in his arms and Anne and others followed with ice buckets.

John shook hands again with the actor and with Harrison and was relieved when Donald approached with glasses of champagne.

"A toast!" Donald yelled, and once everyone had a glass, they all drank a toast to John's success as an artist.

John went to Willy and put his arm around her as they toasted him. He was happy, and he felt that this toast, this unanimous wish of good luck to him by all the people who knew him best, would wipe out any jinx placed on him by the slide show.

Then the formality of the moment passed, and people broke into groups, some coming up to shake John's hand and wish him well, others crowding around the actor. Erica Hart, never one to ignore a good-looking man, was one of the first to be at the actor's side, and John and Willy, standing nearby, could hear him explaining just how the ghost head had worked. Conversation stopped a moment while everyone looked at the powerful miniature cassette he had had strapped to his belt, which had sent out the sounds of creaking and clanking and laughter. The music for the slide show had come from a tape Harrison had made and asked Mark to put in his cassette player, which was hooked to stereo speakers. It was all entirely explainable, and very clever.

Still, when at last all the guests had left, Mark and Anne and Willy and John collapsed with drinks in front of the dying fire, and John confessed that he had not been entirely thrilled by the surprise.

"I didn't know what to do," Anne said. "Harrison called me yesterday and said he had a surprise going-away presentation for you, something he had worked on especially. Mark and I didn't know what to do; we really couldn't refuse."

"I think he hates me," John said.

"Oh, I don't think so," Willy protested.

Mark agreed. "I don't think he hates you at all, John. Perhaps he's just jealous of you. What artist wouldn't be jealous of you, giving up the crass materialistic world to go off and be an honest artist. What you're doing looks noble and brave compared to what he's been doing all his life."

"Still, that's no reason to curse me," John said.

"Oh, John, I really think you're taking this too seriously," Willy said.

"Well, I don't think you're taking it seriously enough!" John snapped.

"I didn't realize you were so superstitious," Willy replied quietly.

"I'm not, Willy," John said. "It's just that—Oh, hell." He couldn't explain.

Willy rose from her chair and crossed the room to snuggle

25

down on the sofa next to John. She touched his arm. "It will be all right," she said. "It really will. You know it will, John. Once we're on our way, it will all be lovely, and someday you'll laugh at tonight."

"She's right, buddy," Mark said. "That old snake doesn't have the power to curse you even if he wanted to. Forget about his stupid slide show. Remember all the stuff you've been told by your teachers and critics and artist friends. You can do it. You're going to do it. God, think of it, John, you're on your own now! You're going to go off and live your dream."

"Yeah," John said, relaxing, grinning. "It really is going to happen."

The four began to talk about plans for the next day then, when the movers would come, when Willy and John would arrive for dinner and to spend the night at the Hunters'.

The fire died down, and the room grew dark. Outside, the wind blew autumn leaves against the windows with little pattering noises. Even though it was late, the four sat talking, not wanting the night to end. They were all enjoying the sense of being on the edge of an adventure while still sheltered safely in the comfort of the warm house and the friendly company.

CHAPTER TWO

WILLY AND ANNE WERE LOOKING OUT THE ATTIC WINDOW down over the rooftops and trees to Nantucket harbor.

"This street," Willy said, "Orange Street, used to be called the captain's lane during the whaling days. The wives of the captains of whaling vessels could look out from their widow's walks to see if a ship was returning to harbor. The next street down, down the hill, was called the first mate's street. Sometimes the husbands were gone for three or four *years*. Imagine it. And then, when they returned home, there were times when the tide wasn't right and they couldn't get into the harbor. The wives could stand on their widow's walks or here, at windows like this one, and look out and *see* the boats waiting to come in."

"I couldn't stand it," Anne replied. Her hands were clasped protectively over her stomach as she stood by Willy's side, looking out. Now almost seven months pregnant, she couldn't get as close to the window as Willy could. "How did they stand it, those women? They must have gone mad."

"Or had affairs with their gardeners." Willy grinned.

"Or with each other." Anne laughed. *"Something."*

"They took laudanum," Willy said. "It's a derivative of opium. The realtor told me. It was a common practice. But when their husbands returned, they were so wealthy, brought back such treasures, silver, Chinese porcelain, ivory, silks . . ."

"Forget all that," Anne said. "I just want Mark in bed with me *every night.* That's all the treasure I want."

"Well, not quite." Willy smiled, looking at Anne's tummy.

"What about you?" Anne said, turning away from the view so she could lean up against the wall. She sighed. With the baby pressing on her, she was always sighing these days. "Willy, you're *thirty.* If you're going to have a baby—"

"There's time," Willy said. She moved close to the window and rested her cheek against the cool pane. Through the filigree of bare tree branches she could see the bright blue water of the harbor. It was filled with small boats, scallopers. "John wants five years to paint. To be really dedicated, committed, uninterrupted. It's necessary to him, Anne. It's the whole point of our move here. You know that."

"Five years," Anne said. She sighed again. "You'll be thirty-five."

"Everyone's having babies late these days," Willy said. "I can get pregnant at thirty-five."

"Maybe," Anne said almost sullenly.

"Oh, you just want everyone to be pregnant because you are," Willy said, tilting her head away from the window and laughing at her friend. "Don't be silly. Don't worry, Anne, we'll have babies. Or maybe we won't. I want children. John wants children, eventually. But first he really wants to work on his art, and you know my priorities. I want John to be happy. I want our marriage to be good. It's been so good for *eight* years now, just think of it. Oh, Anne, it really is something these days to have such a good marriage after eight years. The same with you and Mark—what is it, six years now? Talk about treasures, I think a happy marriage is the ultimate treasure."

"Yes," Anne said. "You're right. We are lucky. We really are lucky."

"And look at this place," Willy said, turning from the window and stretching out her arms. "Won't it be heaven for John to work in? Of course he'll need to put in banks of fluorescent lights. But the space and the wide-board floors and the views . . ."

Anne smugly crossed her arms over her enormous stomach and watched Willy as she moved around the big open attic. Slightly miffed because Willy didn't share her enthusiasm for pregnancy, Anne looked at Willy now with a critical eye.

Willy was such a large woman, as large as her husband, but still graceful and feminine. She had played enough tennis and swum and ridden and skied enough so that she was perfectly at ease with her body. Willy moved through the world with a sort of lovely laziness, as if she never needed to be quick or alert.

Anne secretly thought that Willy had a "midwestern face"—open, honest, healthy, with bright blue eyes and perfect rosy skin and a bland, rather undramatic bone structure. It was the kind of face that makeup couldn't improve; but then it was also the kind of face that the lack of makeup couldn't hurt. She looked as pleasant early in the morning as she did at a party. Her hair was the color of wheat, and it was thick and long; today Willy wore it pulled into an intricate clump at the back of her head. Willy tended to wear jeans and turtlenecks or pleated kilts and wool sweaters; if her face was midwestern, her overall image was more British, Anne thought, like one of those large, comfortable women who train dogs or horses.

And Willy was all those things—open, honest, healthy, pleasant, comfortable, and large. But Anne had to admit that her friend had secrets.

The first Anne had discovered eight years ago when Willy was given introductory passes to a new health spa in Boston. It was an especially cold winter, and Anne jumped at the chance to spend a few hours with Willy one Saturday, swimming, taking a sauna, sitting in the whirlpool, lying in the sun room. Anne didn't know Willy well then; her husband and Willy's had been childhood friends, had gone to B.U. together, but Anne and Willy had met only through their husbands. They had not had a chance to get to know one another. This was a good afternoon, a friendly, warm time when the women had relaxed in the swirling water and discussed freely all sorts of things: their marriage, their pasts, their work.

They used the sun room last and had to take turns at it, and Anne went first. She was in the locker room, getting ready to take a shower and then dress, when Willy walked in from the sun room. She was naked, rosy, and relaxed from the heat, and as she entered, lazy in her nakedness, she reached up with both hands to release her hair from its pins. Her hair fell rich and thick, honey-colored, all around her face and shoulders.

"My God," Anne said, looking at her friend, "no wonder John's so much in love with you. You look like some kind of . . . *goddess.*"

Willy did look like some kind of goddess. Her body, which seemed so *practical,* so plain in clothes, was downright fabulous naked. She was not fat, but she was large and full, with ample hips, long, full thighs, and huge, firm breasts. Her waist was not small—nothing about Willy was small—but it curved in a lovely line from her rib cage in and out again to her hips, something else Anne had not realized because of the shapeless clothes Willy wore.

Willy had smiled at Anne. "Well," she said, only slightly embarrassed, "John likes me. That's what matters."

"But, but," Anne stammered, "how can you be so relaxed about it all? I mean, I'm always worrying about some part of my body, whether I'm too fat or too thin—"

"You're lovely, Anne," Willy had interrupted, moving on into the shower."

"Yes, yes, I know," Anne had replied. "But I'm still always worrying about something. Aren't you? Don't you?"

Willy thought about it as she turned on the water and soaped herself. "I used to," she said. "Oh, of course, in the *teenage* years. What do you think, Anne, imagine how it was, I was always taller, bigger, than most of the boys. And my name! Wilhelmina! Even my nickname which I prefer, isn't pretty. So masculine. It took me a long time to get comfortable with it all, my size, my name, but I just don't even think about it now. You know, since I've married John, I've gotten, well, satisfied with myself. And John certainly seems to be . . . satisfied with me." Willy grinned.

That was Willy's first secret, that in spite of her rather plain appearance she was a marvelous sight naked and so moved through the world with, if not a certain smugness, then a definite calm. She was not much bothered by the opinion of others.

Her other secret was better known: Large Willy did the most delicate, intricate embroidery work on earth.

Anne still was amused at the sight, at the *idea* even, of big, wide Willy, seated so still with an embroidery hoop in her hand or with material stretched over a larger frame, so carefully poking the tiny needle with the slender bright threads in and out. The silver needle looked ridiculous in Willy's large hand. Willy looked silly at her work, like a lumberjack playing with toothpicks, but she didn't know that, or didn't care. She was very content with her craft. Seated in her sewing room, with penciled sketches or designs thumbtacked or taped to the walls and her precious virgin garments hiding in tissue and boxes, waiting to be adorned, and her even more precious brilliant threads and fine needles meticulously arranged in quilted silken boxes, she was in her own kind of paradise.

Several times Anne had dropped in to visit Willy to find her so engrossed in her work that Anne had lounged at the doorway to the sewing room for as long as fifteen minutes. Willy played music while working—Vivaldi or Gershwin or Nielsen, depending on the style of her current design—so she couldn't hear intruders easily. Willy would bend over her frame, intent, poking the needle in, drawing the shining line of thread through, as rapt with her work as a child listening to a fairy tale. At last, bored, Anne would clear her throat, and Willy would turn to her and smile.

"Anne!" she would say. "How nice!" She would rise, her hands filled with rose and turquoise threads, an Amazon with a bouquet of impatiens. "I'm so glad you've come; my back is breaking. Let's have some tea."

That was Willy's second secret, her work, which satisfied her so. Sometimes it put Anne off, this pleasure of Willy's. Anne thought her satisfaction in her work was often a selfish, aloof satisfaction. Willy didn't care if her things sold or if people wrote her letters raving about them. Her pleasures didn't come from outside. It was all interior, all in the work itself. Not much of it could be shared. Willy never spoke about it to Anne, and Anne often felt childishly jealous, slighted. Then she would tell Mark that she thought Willy was too passive.

Now Willy was ranging around the attic, carrying on about what a perfect studio it would make for John, how it would finally give him the chance he'd always wanted to explore his talent. Anne wondered. Artists led risky lives. Anne hoped John would succeed, especially for Willy's sake. She couldn't imagine what would happen if John didn't achieve some kind of success with his art. He was such an emotional man.

"Hey! What are you two doing up there? Come on!" It was John calling them from the doorway at the foot of the wooden steps. "If we don't go for a walk now, it will be too late."

"All right!" Willy called back. "We'll be right down." She switched off the lights and headed for the stairs.

The attic was still bright without the electric lights. It was the day after Thanksgiving, but sunny. The small skylight, which led to the broken and unusable widow's walk on the roof of the attic, was filled with blue sky.

"This is an *interesting* room," Willy said, coming across the attic to go downstairs with Anne. "Don't you think? It *feels* interesting."

"Why don't you take it for yourself?" Anne suggested. "You've got so many rooms in this old house."

"Oh, no," Willy said. "This is by far the largest room, and John will need a large area for his canvases." She gestured to the boxes and crates stacked in one corner. "All those have to be unpacked. I'll be fine in one of the bedrooms. Listen, do you want me to help you down the stairs?"

THE FOUR FRIENDS DROVE OUT TO SURFSIDE AND WALKED ALONG THE beach, which was dramatic that day, with splendid crashing blue-and-white waves. The women walked behind the men, more slowly because of Anne's cumbersomeness, and from time to time Mark could hear Anne carrying on about their Lamaze class, her breathing exercises.

John was going on in detail about the changes that would have to be made in the house: the fluorescent lights he wanted in the attic, the work that would eventually have to be done to modernize the kitchen. The balusters that supported the railing along the high, elegant front stairway from the second floor to the first needed repair. They looked firm but were deceptively weak. Sometimes he had been able to knock them out with only a slight unintentional blow. As he climbed the stairs to bed with a book, for example, he had accidentally, lightly, knocked one wooden post with the book, and the post had teetered, then fallen down to the floor. John guessed that the previous owners had knocked a lot loose when they were moving their furniture out, then fixed them back in with glue, a hasty and shoddy job. Every room in the house needed something. It was an old house, built in 1820, and so would always need repairs. But basically it was strong, sturdy, and tight. Some of the workman-ship was beautiful. John and Willy were planning to strip the painted woodwork around the ornate fireplace in the front room. Perhaps they'd get to it this winter. And they wanted to rebuild the widow's walk, which had been left in disrepair so long that it wasn't safe.

"You never cease to amaze me," Mark said to John. The men had to yell slightly to be heard over the sound of the waves.

John grinned at his friend. "Why?"

"Well," Mark said, "all this house stuff. You never used to care what your . . . abode . . . looked like."

This was true. During the eight years of their marriage, John and Willy had lived in a small but chic apartment on Marlborough Street in Boston. Willy kept the small second bedroom, which she had turned into her sewing room, charmingly neat, and she managed to keep returning the rest of the apartment to some kind of order. But John hadn't cared about any of that, about how the place looked. For him the apartment was only a convenience, a place to toss his clothes and personal necessities while he roamed and thrived out in the real world. John liked being with people. He liked going to the ad agency or the cafés, bars, restaurants, and private clubs where he met his friends and colleagues and clients. And in their college days, when the two men had taken an apartment together their junior and senior years, John's room had been not only sloppy but downright filthy. So this was quite a change, this sudden concern about the niceties of newel posts.

But then John had always been capable of surprising Mark. The two had known each other from childhood, yet John's major life choices had been a shock to Mark every time.

Like marrying Willy. Mark couldn't believe it when John proposed to Willy. Not that Mark didn't like her; he liked her a lot. But she was so damned big. She made John look like a small man in comparison, and he wasn't small. He was five feet ten—as was Willy—but slim, with elegant long bones. And he was handsome in a clean-cut, old-fashioned way, with black hair and blue eyes and a mustache that adorned a smile that made you glad you'd lived to see it. In high school and college he always had had his pick of the girls. He still could. But for some reason, he had chosen Willy and had stayed faithful to her.

Once Mark, who was a lawyer, had stopped by the Blackstone Group to drop off some papers John had left in his car the night before when they had gone to work out at a gym together. Mark had been shown into a large workroom where John was bent over a high table, working on a sketch of a refrigerator with an ice maker in the door. The secretary who showed Mark in had been a sensational redhead with a body that *Playboy* would have loved. She announced Mark's presence with such loving honeyed tones and looked at John with such melting seductiveness that Mark had nearly gotten an erection.

"I really wouldn't blame you for that one," Mark had said to John once the secretary had gone away, shutting the door behind her.

"Huh?" John asked, raising up from the worktable.

"If you had an affair with her," Mark said. "God, John, even a saint couldn't resist that."

"What are you talking about?" John laughed. *"Those* days are over, you old lech. We're married men, remember? Besides, she's only a kid."

"What is she, six years younger than you?"

"Mentally, I mean," John said. "Intellectually. Come on, Mark, give me a break. You know I'd never do that to Willy."

Mark figured maybe it was their careers that caused them to react in such different ways. Mark worked with legal documents, caustic words, angry and frightened people; a good-looking smiling woman always took his breath away. But

John, up there in his ad agency, was surrounded by beauty: beautiful models, beautiful animals, even beautiful machines. Mark supposed that John had gotten used to beauty by now; it just didn't have the same effect on him as it did on other men. He liked it but found it commonplace.

Evidently John found something extraordinary in Willy, because he had married her and stayed faithful to her and remained happy with her for eight years now. Mark had assumed that John was perfectly happy with everything in his life.

But now this move to Nantucket. It had surprised Mark that John would give up a comfortable, even enviable, position with a top ad agency, making top money, in order to move to the isolated little island to try to be an artist. Oh, well, at first it had shocked Mark when John went to work in the inner circles of the agency; it had seemed to Mark that John should have been a salesman. He was so handsome, talkative, likable, witty. People liked John, and Mark had been surprised when John had taken the job doing artwork behind the scenes. Now he had given that up. And he had done it so quickly, as if afraid that if he didn't do it in a flash, he wouldn't do it at all. John had resigned from the agency, bought the house, and moved to Nantucket in three months' time.

"I want more for my life," John was saying now. He had moved away from Mark and was yelling to make himself heard. "I want more for my *soul.* Don't laugh. When I turned thirty, I started thinking. You know, my life's been so fucking *artificial.* All this easy praise and money because I can draw a good likeness of a computer. That's shit. I need more. I need to . . . enrich my life. I don't mean *money* rich."

"Money rich isn't bad," Mark yelled back through the wind, over the sound of the waves. He and John had trouble on this subject sometimes. When John insisted that money didn't matter, Mark reminded him that he could say that only because he had plenty of it—Willy's family money—to fall back on. But John always took that comment as an insult, never managed to see it as a real fact of life: The Hunters had to worry about money, and the Constables didn't.

Now John waved Mark's remark aside. "You know what I mean." He drew closer to Mark, almost bumping into him in his earnestness. "I want—Oh, hell, I want to find out the fucking *meaning of my life*. Don't you understand? Don't you ever want that? Don't you ever want something *special*?"

"Well," Mark said slowly, turning John's question in his mind, "I suppose so. I suppose that's why we're having this baby, you know."

"Yeah," John said. "I can see that. The baby. That wouldn't do it for me right now. But then you're probably not as raving desperate as I am about this, because you're into your work."

"Not any more than you were!" Mark yelled, surprised. "Good god, John, you'd gone to the top."

"Yeah, but you're a *lawyer*. What you do has significance. You help people. You make a difference to their lives." John stopped in his tracks and shook his head. "No," he said, "that's not all I mean. Not just that."

"Sounds like you in your liberal college days." Mark smiled, stopping next to his friend. The women were far back now, sitting in the sand, huddled next to each other with the collars turned up on their coats.

"It's not the other people," John said. "Or not just that. I mean it's great that you help those people. But what I'm trying to get at is that you like what you do. You are what you do. You are *satisfied* by what you do. And I'm not. I can do it, I can make money by it, but it doesn't satisfy me. *Fulfill* me, to use a corny term. I look at Willy sometimes . . ." John turned to gaze back at his wife. "That damned embroidery stuff of hers, well, it doesn't matter one way or the other in the world, in the course of the world, does it? Yet it makes her so *content*. And people are so impressed with her work, they just go crazy over it. The things people say to her, write to her—hell, one woman called her a *visionary.* Willy a visionary." John went quiet. He began to walk again, and Mark walked along beside him for a while.

"I'm not sure you know just what it is you want," Mark said after a while.

"I know," John replied. "I'm not making myself clear. I'm not clear on it myself. I think it is that I want to be an artist. I want fame and praise for what *I can do,* for the way I interpret the world. And I want that—that fucking happiness Willy has—from doing my art. That sense of tapping the juices of the world. A feeling that I'm special. That's what I want. I think."

"I hope you get it," Mark said. "You've invested a lot in this move."

John didn't answer. The two men walked on some more, then turned around to walk back to the women. The beach was empty except for the four friends. Gulls soared overhead, calling to each other. The light was fading in the sky in long streaks, as if the color and clouds were being pulled from the picture by an invisible hand. Everything was shimmering with a muted silver light. Mark was struck by the beauty of this bleak November day, and also a little intimidated by it. This Nantucket shoreline, stripped of sunshine and people, the familiar, now was so raw, so vast.

"I want something *special,*" John said to Mark. "I want to *be* special."

"You're special to a lot of us," Mark said, cuffing his friend on the shoulder, smiling.

John shook his head in despair at explaining but returned the smile.

~~~~~~~

BY NIGHTFALL IT WAS RAINING, AND THE WIND HAD COME UP. THE four friends sat in the high-ceilinged dining room and ate

Thanksgiving-dinner leftovers by candlelight. They lit a fire in the living room fireplace and played a game of Pente, the women against the men.

"I love these little stones," Willy said, fingering her deep blue pebble-sized playing pieces. "They're like jewels."

"Mmm, I know," Anne agreed. "This is a beautiful game. And it seems so ancient. I can believe it really is ancient."

Mark was leaning an elbow on the coffee table, studying the game, pondering his next move.

"What is that warning I get to say?" John asked. "We've got one move, partner, or something like that?"

"Something like that," Willy said.

"Well, I'm saying it," John said.

The wind howled and threw itself against the windows. Now and then the wind made screaming noises, and the windows shook as if someone were trying to get in.

"Some night," Mark said, placing a stone on the board.

"The fire's wonderful," Anne said.

"I'm glad you're enjoying it," John said, smiling. "It cost us enough. We had the movers bring a cord of firewood over on the ferry—there's no timber on Nantucket Island, no trees tall enough for firewood. So a good log is worth its weight in gold. It cost us a thousand dollars to bring over all our stuff, including the wood. Can you believe that?"

"Well," Anne said, "all your furniture's so heavy. All these antiques. They must weigh a ton. But they look wonderful here. They look as if they were meant to be here. Much better than they did in your apartment."

There was a great puffing noise as the wind hit the chimney just the right way to enter the flue and send a gust of smoke back into the room. For a moment rain splattered the logs.

"I don't know," Anne said. "I don't think I could live here all year. I mean, this is only November, and the weather's so wild."

"Well, Nantucket's flat and so far out in the ocean that the wind can really work up some force," John said. "I've heard that it does really blow here. This is nothing."

"I think it's romantic," Willy said smugly.

"I think I'm glad I won't have your heating bill," Mark said just as smugly.

"I think we've beat you." Anne laughed, placing her deep blue stone on a square that gave the women five stones in a row.

"So much for men being superior at logic!" Willy laughed, pleased at winning. She rose. "I'm going to make us all some Irish coffee."

"Oh, great!" Anne said. "I haven't had Irish coffee for years. I don't suppose that much alcohol will hurt the baby, do you, Mark?" She moved over to sit next to her husband on the sofa. "I didn't have any wine with dinner tonight."

"My sweet, you drink just enough booze to make our child into a *bon vivant* and not enough to turn him into a drunk," Mark said, pulling Anne closer to him and rubbing her stomach.

John put the colored stones back in their bag, rolled up the Pente mat, and put the game away. He rose and dropped another log on the fire. The friends sat together in silence for a while, relaxing, stretching out, watching the dancing flames. They were familiar enough with each other to be companionable in silence. For a few minutes the whir of the electric mixer as Willy whipped the cream for the Irish coffee joined the other noises of the night. It had a nice controlled mechanical sound about it—a civilized sound—and when she turned it off, the storm outside seemed even more savage by contrast.

"I'm glad I'm not on the ferry," Mark said, making seasick noises and faces.

"It may not be running tonight," John told him. "I've heard it doesn't go when it's really bad."

Willy entered the room carrying a silver tray with four crystal goblets filled with Irish coffee and four long silver spoons. She was wearing jeans and an old cotton turtleneck and an even older gray-and-heather cable-knit wool sweater she had knit herself years before. She looked enormously comfortable and warming, and with the silver tray in her hands, she was a bearer of gifts. She set the tray on the coffee table, and everyone looked at the Irish coffees, which she had prepared perfectly, so that the white cream rose in swirls, sweet islands on dark, intoxicating seas.

Anne clapped her hands together like a child. "Oh," she cried, "this is such a luxury! The walk and the waves and the wild beach, and now this fire and this rich dessert. Willy, you're wonderful."

Willy smiled. "Well, it's a luxury for *us,*" she said. "To have friends in our house. We don't know anyone here, you know. I mean, we know the realtor. And there are some people in Boston who come here for the summer, but no one we know stays for the entire year. Imagine, we really don't know a *soul* on this island."

Anne shivered. "I'd hate it. I'd feel desolate. Willy, I couldn't stand it."

"Well," Willy said, picking up her coffee, "it's only been three weeks. I'm sure we'll be meeting people as time goes along."

"I don't want to," John announced. "I have no desire whatsoever to meet anyone. I want privacy, peace, and quiet."

"Sounds drastic to me," Mark told him. "Too much of a change too fast. John, you've lived your life surrounded by people. You love people, admit it."

"I admit it," John said. "But I also never got any work done. I want to get some work done. Some real work."

The wind shrieked. The windows shook. Rain splattered against the panes like pebbles thrown from an unseen hand.

"You'll get your work done," Willy said to her husband.

"I have to," John said soberly.

Anne and Mark looked at each other.

"Well," Mark said, a little more loudly than necessary, thinking quickly, wanting to change the subject, "tell me, do you two have a ghost in your house? I hear Nantucket's supposed to be full of ghosts."

"Ghosts!" John laughed, his good humor immediately returning. "In spite of your Halloween party, my friend, I don't believe in ghosts. No one believes in ghosts anymore."

"Oh, I don't know," Willy said. She was slowly stirring her cream into the coffee-and-whiskey mixture, making hypnotic whorls of brown and white. "The other day we drove out to the moors and took a long walk. The moors are beautiful now, even with most of the color gone. There are bayberries, low bushes, twisted trees, different mosses, everything now olive and dark green and gray, with vivid spots of deep-wine-colored berries here and there. The moors undulate slightly"—Willy dipped her hand slowly—"and there are shallow hollows in the low hills. We stood on a high spot for a while and watched the mist pass through, and honestly, Anne, the way those mists wafted and drifted along—they seemed like spirits. Didn't they, John? They really seemed human. Or at least alive."

"Just looked like fog to me," John said to his wife, watching her with affection.

"And then the foghorn," Willy went on. "It's so melancholy. So haunting. Like a warning from a lost soul. . . . 'Go . . . go . . . no . . . you must not come here . . . go.' . . .'" Willy drew out the last word as if it were a deep musical note.

"God, Willy, this island's making you weird!" Anne snapped, shuddering.

"Willy's always been weird," John said, and reached over to lightly caress his wife's neck to show her he was kidding. He leaned back in his chair with his Irish coffee in his hands and put his feet up on Willy's lap.

"I resemble that remark!" Willy said, laughing, making a

familiar joke between the two of them to show she wasn't hurt. "But really," she went on, "I wouldn't mind if we did have a ghost. I could have a friend!"

"Honestly," Anne said. "Willy, you are always so *optimistic.* Isn't she, John? Doesn't it just drive you crazy sometimes? I mean, give me a break, Willy, ghosts aren't people's *friends.* They're evil spirits, they're malign."

"*Pol-ter-geist,*" Mark said, naming a movie they had all seen together, making his voice deep and ominous as he said the word.

"Yeah," Anne agreed.

"Well, who says ghosts have to be evil?" John asked, more to come to his wife's rescue than because he cared.

"Everyone!" Anne answered. "Everyone knows that, John. Ghosts are spirits of people who are not satisfied with what happened to them on earth. They're angry, or sad—that's why they're ghosts. They can't be at peace, and so they moan around wherever it was they were made unhappy, haunting people and trying to get some kind of revenge."

"You see too much TV," John said.

"No. No, now *really,*" Anne said earnestly, sitting up as straight as she could, "look at it this way. I've got a *human being* in here," she said, pointing to her swollen belly. "A person with his or her own special characteristics, his or her own personality—spirit—someone we've never met before, someone who has never existed before. But does exist now. I've got a very small human being inside me; we all believe that. No one doubts that. So if we can believe that from out of nowhere came this new human to live for a while in my tiny space, why can't we believe that in all the vast universe there are spirits, human beings in other forms, forms we don't know about, who also exist?"

The other three in the room were quiet, surprised and a little embarrassed by Anne's unexpected passion.

"We can find empirical evidence that babies exist in women's bellies," John began. He spoke hesitantly, gently, as if he were afraid of insulting her. "Babies come out of women's wombs. If we cut women open, we find babies in there. Now we can film, live, babies *in utero.* I don't think that mankind, in general, over time, has ever had the same sort of evidence that spirits live an afterlife. The same sort of proof that ghosts exist."

"I think we all *want* to believe in ghosts," Willy agreed. "The same way we want to believe there's a God. But I think John's right. There just isn't enough evidence to prove that ghosts exist."

"Oh, hormones," Anne said. Then, seeing the confusion on the others' faces, she laughed, and the mood of the room lightened. "I *mean,* it's my hormones, this pregnancy, that gets me into such a state. All worked up and sentimental and so *concerned.* So mystical and romantic. I'm sorry, you guys."

"We should go to bed," Mark said. "It's late, and you need your sleep," he told his wife.

"It's true," Anne agreed. She smiled at the others. "I have to stay in bed nine hours to get eight hours of sleep because the baby always wakens me several times a night, kicking. It kicks Mark, too, if he's lying close enough to me."

"Well, have a good sleep," Willy said. "It's still vacation tomorrow, sleep as late as you can."

Mark and Anne went upstairs. Willy and John stayed by the fire.

"You envy Anne, don't you," John asked Willy, watching her face.

"What?" Willy asked. "What do you mean?"

"I mean the baby. You wish you could be having a baby, too. I saw your face when you looked at her stomach."

Willy rose and went over to her husband. She knelt beside him and wrapped her arms around his legs and laid her head on his knees. "John," she said, "of course I want a baby. Sometime.

There's no hurry. I can wait. I've told you that. I want *you*. I want *us*. I want us to be happy. I've got what I want, really. Believe me."

"I love you, Willy," John said.

She smiled and nestled against his legs while he stroked her dark blond hair. They stayed that way for a long time. Willy closed her eyes and gave over to the sensation of John's gentle hands on her hair. John caressed his wife and stared into the fire, wondering if he could ever be as content as she was. Outside their circle of warmth and light and love, the wind and rain rampaged in the dark night.

CHAPTER THREE

EARLY SUNDAY AFTERNOON WILLY AND JOHN DROVE ANNE AND
Mark to the airport to catch their flight back to Boston. When
they returned to their house, it seemed much emptier to them
than it had before their friends' visit. It seemed so quiet.
Outside, a fine cold rain descended very steadily, slipping down
along the walls of the houses and escaping downhill in rivulets.
Inside, the house was cold, the fireplace dark with mounds of
ashes.

They turned on all the electric lights and turned up the
heat. Soon their oil-fired hot-air furnace was making its predict-
able, companionable blowing sounds. But still they could not
get settled in their house. The *New York Times* and the *Boston
Globe* lay in scattered piles all over the living room floor. The
four friends had read the papers in the morning, drinking coffee
and interrupting each other to read some item aloud, laughing
or making comments. These papers, which always filled Willy
and John with a kind of greed and hunger when they were
picked up in the morning, fresh with smeary ink, now seemed

46

just messy. So did the coffee cups and plates that had held their late-morning brunch of coffee, ham and cheese croissants, and green grapes. Crumbs and small brown stems littered the plates; cold coffee lay murky in the cups.

It didn't take long to clean up the mess. They carried the dirty dishes into the kitchen and rinsed and stacked them in their dishwasher; they piled the papers on the back porch. John ran a dust cloth over the coffee table and set the furniture back at its formal angles. And still the house wasn't right. The windows held no welcoming change of scene; only a grim light that struggled through the thick clouds and rain-dense air. And it was late November, they were headed toward the winter solstice, so night would fall early.

"Anything on TV?" John asked, sitting on the sofa, stretching his legs out before him.

" 'Masterpiece Theater,' " Willy answered. "At nine."

They both looked at their watches, even though they could guess what time it was: only a little after one o'clock.

"There's an hour-long Alfred Hitchcock at six," Willy said. "That might be fun."

"All right," John agreed. "Or we could go out to eat."

"Oh, let's," Willy said. "I'm tired of cooking. Let's go pig out at the Atlantic Cafe and then come home and read and watch TV."

John agreed, but still the afternoon lay before them.

"You know what it is?" Willy said, perching in a chair facing her husband, sticking her hands into the pockets of the caramel-colored down vest she often wore. "It's that we don't have any workers in the house or about to arrive. The first three weeks people were always showing up; the movers with the furniture, the carpenters and the mason, and so on. There was all that rushing around trying to decide where to put the linens and unpacking the china and rearranging the sofas, and as soon as we got that done, we rushed around getting ready

47

for Thanksgiving, and the Hunters arrived. Now we're really moved in."

"Mmm," John said. A familiar sulkiness was settling over him, an old childhood reaction to boredom. He vaguely wanted to argue or complain. "We shouldn't have done this," he said. "I probably made an enormous mistake. Moving us here. Giving up my job. Part of what I feel today is because I know I don't have anywhere to go tomorrow. No office, no friends, no schedules or commitments. All the days are going to seem the same from now on."

"Nonsense," Willy said, smiling. She didn't mind coaxing him away from the doldrums; he did this for her regularly, once a month, when she was premenstrual. "You're going to make a schedule for yourself. And you're going to paint. You're going to work. You've been waiting for this for a long time."

She moved over to the sofa and cuddled next to her husband. "It's bound to take some time to get started. You can't expect it to happen all at once. There can't be the same sense of furious activity that goes on at the agency, where there are so many people. So it will seem like everything's happening super slowly. But you will be able to work, John. I know it. I'm sure of it. And just think," she went on, snuggling closer, "you'll have a freedom you never had before. I mean, if you want to stop working, if you should get some kind of uncontrollable urge . . ." She nibbled on his ear and down his neck as she talked. She ran her hand under his sweater and began to unbutton his shirt. "We'll have the luxury of long afternoons together. . . ." she whispered, nuzzling her head against his chest.

But Willy had started John thinking about his work, and he was suddenly restless with a need to get up to the attic, to start *being* there, thinking about what he wanted to do.

John took both his wife's hands in his and kissed them. "I love you, Willy," he said. "I don't know what I'd do without you." He pushed her away from him gently. "Look," he said, "I want to go up to the attic for a while now. Just because it's Sunday doesn't mean I can't work. I just want to go up for a while and think about where to start. Okay?" He kissed her forehead; Willy was making a pouty face, but he could tell by her eyes that she was kidding. "Listen," he said, "you're the one who started me thinking about my work. It's your fault."

"Mmm," Willy said, pushing herself up off the sofa and stretching. "It's all right. And you're right—you're free now to paint whenever you want. Sundays, evenings—in the middle of the night if you want. You don't have to wake up early for work or be fresh for the office. It's really kind of marvelous when you think about it. Well, do go on up for a while. I think I'll get a start on my holiday fruitcakes. It's a good day for baking."

John sat on the sofa and watched his wife walk through the dining room and into the kitchen. Every year she baked rich, moist cakes laced with bourbon and brilliant with jewellike green-and-red cherries, and with dates and nuts. She sent these off to their distant older relatives and to the friends who especially liked fruitcakes. She and John seldom ate it them-selves. But Willy liked making fruitcakes. Liked having them sit wrapped in silver foil, secretly growing darker, richer, each day. Liked sending handmade gifts to friends. John envied Willy. There seemed no end to the pleasurable tasks she thought up for herself. Already she was humming carols softly to herself as she moved around the kitchen, setting out the ingredients. She was better at solitude than he.

But he could learn. He would learn. He hoisted himself up off the sofa and tromped up the two flights of stairs to the attic.

The large open attic ran the entire length and width of the house; it was thirty feet wide and seventy feet long, for their house was long and narrow. The stairs leading from the first to second floor were decorated with nicely turned balustrades and a rather ornately carved walnut newel post; the steps them-selves were dark-stained walnut, carpeted by the previous owners in a slate blue. At the top of the stairs a long hallway began, leading to the three bedrooms and bathroom. At the front of the hall was a large window looking down onto Orange Street and a doorway leading to the more primitive stairs to the attic.

These were unstained boards of no particular excellence. The attic had unstained wide-board floors, unpainted wide-board walls, and great stretches of white Sheetrock covering the insulation that had been put in the attic ceiling. At the front of the attic was one large window looking down over Orange Street, and at the back was a window of similar size that gave a view of the hill slanting down to the harbor, with its large and small boats. John had put his easel near this window, not for the light so much as for the view, which would be restful to his mind and eyes. In the middle of the attic there was a sort of built-in wooden ladder of nine very wide wooden steps that led in a steep incline to the widow's walk. The former owners had replaced the original door to the widow's walk with a skylight, so that the attic, even on this dark day, was filled with a gentle illumination.

Small raindrops fell in random splatters on the roof and skylight, blown only now and then by gusts of wind. The effect was of birds walking on the roof or small animals moving around inside the walls. John wondered if there were animals in the walls—mice, rats. They had found a dead rat in their driveway last week, and Willy, who was usually sensible, had freaked out. Now she wanted very much to get a cat, and John was trying to find one to give her for Christmas. Unfortunately, this didn't seem to be the season when cats had their litters. He wasn't having much luck.

John perched on the high stool he often used while painting. There was still so much that needed to be done up here. The electrician who was to put in the banks of fluorescent lights had come once, then disappeared and now didn't return the call John left on his answering machine. The carpenter, who had promised to build some shelves to hold John's paints and supplies, had also never come back. But the realtor had laughed when John called to ask him about it.

"There is no unemployment on Nantucket," the realtor told him. "For every plumber and carpenter and electrician on Nantucket, there are fifty families desperate for their services. Besides, they like to go off scalloping. People say there are two speeds here: slow and stop. They'll get around to you sooner or later. Don't take it personally. You'll just have to learn to relax about it."

Relax. John looked around the attic. His paints and brushes and chalks and new canvases were still in cardboard boxes, and he couldn't unpack them unless he wanted to put them right on the floor. Eight naked electric bulbs hung from cords with pull chains at various spots in the attic, so that the lighting was fine, if a little primitive, for normal living but too filled with shadows and dark hollows for painting. And it was cold, John realized. There was no heat in the attic at all. If he left the door from the second floor open at the bottom of the stairs, some heat would rise from the rest of the house. But he would have to get some space heaters if he wanted to stay up here for any length of time.

He stepped down from his stool, found a scratch piece of paper, and began making a list. Perhaps he would bring a radio up here, perhaps a stereo. Willy liked listening to music while she worked; perhaps he would, too. It would be very quiet here after working at the Blackstone Group, whose offices were filled with talk and noise or whispers or at least the sounds of other people moving around.

Space heaters, he wrote. Stereo. Trees topped? Willy had suggested this when they moved in, because she loved a water view. With this window as a frame, only the top third of the picture showed blue water, harbor, and the curving sands of Coatue and Monomoy. The rest of the picture, the majority of it, was filled with rooftops, backyards, winding lanes, picket fences, and the intricate tangle of branches, twigs, and limbs of the old maple trees that grew in their backyard. If the trees were topped, they could get a clearer view of harbor and sky. If not, they would pretty much lose their water view in the summer when the leaves were out.

John turned a page on his sketch pad and began to pencil in the twisting, delicate lines of the trees. The trunks and larger branches were knobby, the smaller branches shot off in odd angles from the center, making awkward turns until the smallest twigs stuck out their dried buds like a child's stick-figure drawing of fingers on a hand.

He sketched rapidly, with a sense of determination filling him and a hint of the feeling of joy that came upon him when he was happy with his work. It was this, after all, that he wanted to capture—it was for this that he had come to Nantucket. He had come to find the natural, the awkward, the awry, the real. His mind, his eye—his soul—were tired of the perfect symmetry and glaring artificial brightness of color in the ads he worked on. He longed for the stunted, the stubby, the muted, the cracked. He wanted to capture the beauty of such things, of these tangled boughs or of the leaves that had fallen from them, which once were green and pliable and now lay shriveled, brittle, and brown, piled by the wind against the fence. All this was as much a part of any human being's life as the perfect. These bare trees, dry leaves, were as beautiful and as valuable as any almond-sided refrigerator or eye shadowed, rouged, and lipsticked model. If he could capture this truth . . .

He drew on, exhilarated. Slowly the light faded from the sky so that at last he could not see even the branches of the trees nearest to him. Night had fallen.

He put down his sketch pad and found the one he had taken with him to the beach the previous week. He had made brief, rough drawings of the ocean, a sailboat, a gull riding on the wind. But the drawing that pleased him the most now was one of pebbles, shells, and seaweed cast up on the shore. In any given square foot of beach, the variety and subtlety of shape and color were amazing. He had not had his paints with him but had scribbled in the colors he wanted to duplicate and drawn arrows from the word to the appropriate shell or stone: coral, dun, peach, plum, washed gray, pale brown, faded blue. Most colors had been dulled by the weathering of sand and sea. He had walked along the shoreline a long way before the dark dappling of stone and shell was broken by one small rock covered by seaweed. The seaweed was still alive, and it was a brilliant emerald green, streaming over the rock and down toward the sea like a woman's hair. That hair . . . John flipped over to a clean sheet of paper and began to sketch. Long, thick, streaming dark hair flowed across his page; he was drawing the woman's head from the back, and he could get only the faintest suggestion of a profile turned toward him. The profile, the face, wasn't important now; only the thick, abundant, streaming dark hair mattered.

John glanced up at the darkened attic window and saw a woman there, just on the other side of the glass.

A young woman in a black cape, her back to him, her profile obscured by the waves of dark hair that streamed down from her head, around her shoulders, to her waist, was out there in the air.

Startled, he dropped his pencil on the floor, and the clatter it made as it hit the wooden boards was immense.

"What the hell?" John said.

The woman in the window disappeared. The window was blank, black.

John rubbed his hands over his eyes. He looked at his watch. It was after five. He had been working for over four hours, and he was exhausted. This had happened to him before—not a hallucination but the same plunge from intense

53

euphoria to sudden, complete fatigue. It was like being dropped from the high of a drug. He was more pleased than frightened by his hallucination—how vivid it had been!—and it seemed to him that this meant that he was really starting to work now, that he was at last beginning to tap into his true artistic core.

He was immensely happy. He shuffled his papers and pads back into order and got ready to go downstairs. He couldn't wait to share all this with Willy, to tell her how well his work had gone. On the first day! He wanted to share his sense of achievement with her, knowing that she would be happy for him.

He wouldn't tell her about the hallucination, though. It had been so brief, so strange—Willy might take it too seriously. Or, worse, not seriously enough. No, he wouldn't mention the hallucination to Willy. He had always envied her her sense of self-sufficiency, of being lost in another world, when she was at work on her embroidery. Her sense of having secrets. Well, now he had his secrets, too. He went down the attic steps and reached up to pull the chain that switched the last light off.

EVEN THOUGH IT WAS RAINING, WILLY AND JOHN WALKED TO THE Atlantic Cafe. The cobblestone streets seemed polished by the sheen of rain in the lamplight, and strangers passed each other with collars turned high, hats pulled low, looking like spies in the night. The inside of the restaurant was cozy and bright by contrast. The bar at the front of the café was lined with fishermen, scallopers, and carpenters, bearded young men with their wool caps stuck in the pockets of their rain slickers, laughing heartily, the storm outside forgotten in the first taste of beer. Willy and John took a booth in the back.

They ordered cheese nachos, zucchini sticks, chicken fingers, cheeseburgers, and dark draft beers, their hunger strong because of their walk in the rain. Willy had braided her long honey-colored hair, and it hung over her shoulder against her thick wool sweater like a rope.

"I saw our carpenter up there at the bar," Willy said. "Although perhaps I'm being too optimistic when I say *our*."

"I didn't see him," John said. "Which one? Beauregard?"

"Yeah," Willy said. "I wonder if one of us should go over and say hello . . . remind him that he promised to be back last week with an estimate for the work."

"I don't know, Willy," John said. "I hate to bother someone on a Sunday night when he's relaxing."

"Well"—Willy sighed—"I suppose you're right. It's just so frustrating, though. There's so much I'd like to have done to the house."

"I know," John agreed. The waitress put their food down in front of them, and for a while they ate in silence. Then John said, "I'd like the skylight fixed so we can use it like a door. Or a hatch. So we can get out on the widow's walk. In fact, I'd like it done right away."

Willy looked up from her food. "Why on earth do you want to get out on the widow's walk?" she asked.

"I don't know exactly," John said, almost as surprised as Willy. They hadn't put the widow's walk at the top of their list before. "It's just that after working up there all afternoon, I feel I need access to it. I want to be able to go in and out on it. Perhaps," he went on, trying to explain to his wife and himself, thinking aloud, "perhaps, it's that I want to get away from the man-made in my work and get back into the natural elements. If I could just go out whenever I wanted to and stand on the widow's walk and feel the wind or rain . . ." He was quiet a moment. "It will be a long time until the spring, until the weather's good enough for me to take my paints outdoors. With the widow's walk accessible, I'll be able to be more in touch with the weather and with what I want to do."

Willy smiled at her husband. "You started working today. Isn't that great?"

"I did start," he said. "Willy, I'm excited about it. I didn't think I'd be able to start—*really* start—so soon."

"Well," Willy said, "let's get that skylight open as soon as we can."

"I love you, Willy," John said.

"I love you," Willy answered. She ate awhile, then began to tell John her plans for painting and carpeting her sewing room. She could do the painting herself; she wanted the walls to be a bright apricot color and the woodwork trimmed in cream; did that sound too odd? They discussed their plans for the house and had hot-fudge sundaes for dessert and finally forced themselves back out into the rain for the walk home.

Back in the house, Willy put on her nightgown and robe and made a pot of decaffeinated coffee for them to drink while they watched "Masterpiece Theater." Then they watched a goofy comedy on HBO, and it was after midnight when they got ready for bed.

"We don't have to set an alarm!" Willy said, crawling into bed next to her husband. "You don't have to leave for work in the morning. Oh, what a luxury. We can sleep as late as we want in the morning."

"So we can stay up as late as we want at night," John said, turning to Willy. He pulled her toward him, feeling her generous curves through her flannel nightgown. "Doing whatever decadent things we want," he went on. "He-he-he," he laughed in a dirty-old-man voice, nuzzling Willy on the neck.

Willy wrapped her arms around his shoulders, but loosely, so that she would not constrain him in his movements. By now they knew each other well enough to know exactly how to give the greatest pleasure. Although for Willy, just *this*—holding her husband in her arms—was the greatest pleasure. She found the current rage described by magazines for women to achieve orgasm amusing, ridiculous, even irritating. Usually, often, she had an orgasm, or several, when she and John made love, but that was not what was important or even best about their lovemaking. The best of it was John in her arms, moving against her, the two of them together; the scratchiness of his evening's beard against her forehead; her lips pressed against his naked shoulder, tasting salt, smelling sweet sweat and the lingering fragrance of clean cotton; the weight of him all up and down her. Often she tried *not* to become orgasmic so that she could focus on this, on John in her arms, his labor against her, the sense of urgency in him. He became everything to her then, her child, her hero, and when she held him in her arms, naked, full-length, on their bed, she was always overcome with a love for him that was so strong that she knew she would kill for him, do anything for him. This was what her life was about. She loved her husband as her heart loved its blood.

THE NEXT FEW DAYS ALMOST GAVE THEM SUMMER BACK. NANTUCKET was nearer the Gulf Stream than the continent and so was often warmer, and for the week after Thanksgiving, the temperature reached fifty-five or sixty almost every day. It was unusual, but Willy and John were delighted.

John took his sketch pad and pencils and inks off in their Wagoneer to different spots on the moors or along the beach and spent entire days sketching and painting. Willy packed him sack lunches of corned beef sandwiches on bread slathered with mustard and thick with sweet onions; she thought onions guarded against catching colds. She added an apple, a beer, a thermos of coffee.

John left by nine every morning and didn't return until five or so at night, and he returned exhilarated, the back of the Wagoneer filled with sketches and small watercolor scenes. It was just picture-postcard stuff, he knew—a canvas of the ferry *Uncatena* rounding Brant Point or of the glaze of bright sun on the smooth water of a pond—but these pictures were a start, a way of feeling his way toward what it was he really wanted to do.

Willy stayed home, threw open the windows, put all her Wyndham Hill records on her stereo, and painted her sewing room. She painted the woodwork cream, the walls a golden-pinkish apricot. The walls were old and had as many wrinkles and eccentricities as an old sailor's face. Former owners had made holes to hang pictures or put in a flue; more recent ones had plastered over or put on wallboard compound and not sanded down thoroughly, leaving lumps and blotches. There were some long wandering cracks that had been there so long they seemed essential to the wall; the wall was not weakened by them. They were just there. Willy didn't mind.

Kirk Beauregard arrived and took measurements for turning the skylight into a hatch that would open onto the widow's walk. He said he'd be back by the end of the week, but he wasn't. It didn't upset the Constables very much; nothing could during this week of kind weather. On Saturday they bundled up in layers and biked out to Surfside together with lunches and paperbacks in their bike baskets and spent the whole day walking on the beach, picnicking in the dunes, watching the ocean tease the shore. Gulls dipped overhead, and families with children and dogs went past, playing games with the surf. Willy and John congratulated themselves for their happiness.

On Sunday, Willy thought she might go to one of the churches on the island but didn't get up in time. She spent the long morning reading the *Times* and the *Globe* and drinking coffee with John. It was cooler today but still sunny. Windy. John wandered off up into the attic to sort through his week's work and start making some kind of order out of his material. Willy curled on the sofa with a book and pulled an afghan up over her. She was too lazy to build a fire.

John sorted through his stuff. He wasn't going to have shelves for months; that was becoming obvious. If he waited on the shelves, he'd never get anything done. The former owners had left behind a large wooden cable wheel in the attic. It stood only about two feet high and was stamped in yellow on its green surface: American Insulated Wire Corp. Pawtucket R.I. But it was sturdy, and John unpacked some of his paints and brushes and set them on that. There was also, in the corner, a heavy old humidifier. It was useless, but as a surface it was *something*, so John stacked some jars and bottles and tins on it. He put his bare canvases and sketch pads along one wall of the attic, and the ones he had been working on during the week he ranged along the back of the attic, so that they were the first things he saw when he came up the stairs. They were not great, but they were passable. Nice scenes that a tourist might pay a few bucks for. This was not what he wanted to do, but it was a step away from microwave ovens.

He found on the floor by his stool the large sketch pad he had been working on the previous Sunday. He flipped through it, then sat thinking. He roamed around the attic for a while, fiddling with the lights; until an electrician showed up, he would have to make do with what lighting he could rig up himself. So he began to fasten the 100-watt bulbs he had bought during the week into the extra hanging sockets that existed at random around the attic. The result was not elegant but bright. It would do till the electrician came.

At some point during the week he had thrown his wool vest up into the attic. Now he remembered why. He dug into the pocket of the vest and found three gull feathers, white tipped with gray; one scallop shell, unbroken, the ridges peach colored, the channels white as snow; one shriveled rose hip, still vividly red. He arranged these carelessly against the rough gray-and-white plaid wool of his vest and began to work. He wanted to capture the different textures of soft feather, fragile shell, dimpled fruit, and their similarities: their delicate curving textured reality. He made some sketches on his pad, then set up his easel and began to work on a large canvas. The barbs of the feathers grew from the shaft with the minute perfection of cat's teeth; he remembered he must look for a kitten for Willy. Then he grew lost in his work.

It was dark outside when he gave up for the day. John sat down on his stool, his arms hanging at his side, considering his work. It was almost half-finished. The penciled outlines were there, and the beginnings of color. He was delighted. And tired, tired in a pleasant, fulfilled way, like a runner who has reached his destination. After a while he rose and went around the attic turning off the light bulbs one by one until the only light remaining was the one hanging over the stairs that was reached from the bottom of the stairs by the pull chain. Now he realized how very quiet the house had become. There were no sounds of Willy fixing dinner, no sounds of music. There came over him the sensation that he was alone in the house now, that Willy had gone out for some reason—to buy groceries? But he felt that she was gone. He was physically exhausted from painting for so long, and he was content. It was dark outside now, and the wind was coming up, rattling the windows.

John stood for a moment, looking out the window toward the harbor, before he realized what he was really looking for. Then he made a gruff noise in his throat, a sort of snort of laughter at himself. He'd been halfway expecting to see some kind of hallucination in the window again, for he had been working very hard. But there was nothing there now. He shook his head at his foolishness and went down the stairs, pulling the chain to switch off the last light.

At the bottom of the stairs he paused. The house was quiet, but in the attic there was a persistent thumping now that he hadn't noticed before. A gentle knocking noise.

Without turning on the light, he went back up into the attic. He stood a moment, listening. Again he wondered if there were creatures in the wall. He really must see about that cat. It sounded as if something wounded were trying to get in. He moved toward the window cautiously, trying to locate the direction of the pattering. There was nothing at the window, although every few moments it shook slightly from the blows of the now forceful wind.

The noise seemed to be coming from the skylight. John reached out and tugged on the chain hanging over the stairs, switching on the light so that the attic was slightly brightened. He wasn't brave enough to encounter some kind of rabid bat or pigeon (he thought of Hitchcock's *Birds*) in the dark.

He walked across the attic to the wide wooden staircase that led steeply up to the skylight. It was the skylight that was being battered. He began to climb the steps, which ascended so sharply that he was practically lying facedown on them. He had to crane his neck backward to look up.

He had gone up three steps, so that his face was nearly against the skylight, when he saw her.

The light from the stairwell was not sufficient to illuminate her clearly, but still he could see without any doubt that she was there.

John saw quite distinctly a young woman with a pale face leaning down over the skylight, her dark cloak billowing heavily against her, her long black hair streaming upward, backward, all around her face in the wind. Her dark eyes were large and beseeching. Her small white hands were making the sounds he had heard: She was beating her palms against the glass. There was no color to her: Her skin was all white, her eyes and hair and cloak all deep black.

"Jesus Christ," John whispered. He clutched the wooden step in front of him. He was dizzy with shock. He had not felt such a deep plunge of fear and dread since he was a child. But he could not seem to look away, and the woman did not disappear. She continued to beat with her small hands on the skylight glass.

"Who are you?" John whispered. But he spoke more to

himself than to the woman at the skylight. In any case, she did not seem to hear him. I'm going mad, John thought. I'm going fucking mad. I think there's a woman blowing around on the roof.

"WILLY!" John yelled.

"No!" the ghost-woman called, and raised a hand, palm out to him, as if to forestall him.

He heard her voice then quite clearly. It was high, light, sweet, enchanting even in its demand. He heard it as clearly as he had ever heard anything.

John stared hard at the woman. She seemed to be kneeling on the roof, bending over the skylight—that much was realistic about her; a real woman could find purchase on the roof like that. And he could see her so clearly: her long hair blowing in the wind, the heavy cape buffeting against her, the contrast between her pale skin and dark eyes. She did not look like a ghost or skeleton or a spirit; she looked like a real woman.

A very beautiful woman.

"Who are you?" John asked again, louder now. He had to speak through teeth he had clenched against the shaking that had overtaken his body. "What are you doing out there? How can you be out there?"

She answered: "Let me in."

"I can't," he said. "The skylight doesn't open. Come to a door."

But she was gone.

In an instant she had vanished. Not moved away, not walked, or flew or fell away; she had simply, completely, disappeared. Like a flame going out on a match. He was left lying against the stairs, his hands growing cold from the chill of the glass.

John knew that either he was going mad or he had seen a ghost. He did not believe in ghosts. But he desperately wanted not to be mad. He rested his head against the step.

After a while an ache ran down his arms into his shoulders. He backed down the steps from the skylight, looking around him as he did. Now the windows were clattering, but only from the wind. Nothing in the attic moved. John went down the stairs to the second floor, switched off the light, and shut the door. He leaned against it and looked around.

Here was the hall leading to the big bedroom at the back of the house that he and Willy shared, to the middle bedroom, now Willy's sewing room, to the guest bedroom at the front of the house and the stairs to the first floor. Here was the reality of worn carpet, light switches, unpacked cartons, familiar furniture. John was still trembling all over. He needed to talk with Willy. He went down the stairs rapidly.

Willy had fallen asleep on the living room sofa with the television turned down low. A football game was ending, and the time was clicking off with digital speed in the right-hand corner of the screen. Willy lay sprawled on the sofa, covered with a multicolored afghan. She was so colorful, even in her sleep, so sane and vivid and *sensible*. Her braided hair, her clean-scrubbed face, her healthy deep breathing, all signs of a peaceful inner life.

John knelt beside his wife. "Willy," he said. "Wake up. Willy, I need you."

Willy woke up almost instantly in that way she had, so that it seemed she had no dream life to push through in order to get back to reality. She sat up and leaned against the sofa arm. "John, what's wrong?"

John took both Willy's hands in his. "Willy, I saw a ghost. Don't laugh," he demanded, because immediately she began to smile. "I'm not kidding. I wish I were kidding. I saw a fucking goddamned ghost."

"Where?" Willy asked. "What was it like?" She pulled her knees up so that John could sit next to her on the sofa.

"I had just finished working. I heard noises—a window

63

being tapped on, but louder than tapping. I climbed the steps to the skylight, and there she was."

"A woman?" Willy asked.

"A young woman," John said. "Wearing a heavy black cloak. She had long black hair. She was trying to get in. She wanted to get in. She asked me to let her in."

"She *spoke* to you?"

"Yes," John said. "Oh, Christ, Willy!" he exclaimed then, and pushed himself up off the sofa. He began to pace the room, his body restless now with the remains of his fear. "I know this sounds crazy. I know it sounds unbelievable. But it happened. I swear it. In fact, it happened last week, too. I had just finished working, and I looked out the harborside window, and I saw a woman there, her back to me. She was the same woman, I'm sure of it, though I didn't see her face. She had lots of black hair and that heavy cape."

"She was just sort of *floating* in the air outside the window?" Willy asked.

"Willy, this is not a joke!" John shouted.

Willy rose and went to her husband. She put her hands on his chest. "I'm not saying it's a joke. I'm not acting like this is a joke," she said. "I was just asking a question."

John looked down. "No, she didn't *float*. She was just there. Standing there. *I* know there's nothing out there for her to stand on. Christ. That's why I didn't tell you last week. I thought I was hallucinating. I thought I'd been working too hard. Too fast. But tonight—Willy, she was there. I saw her. I heard her speak."

"Well, I think this is exciting!" Willy said. "Let's go back up. Let's go see if we can see her."

"Let me fix myself a scotch first," John said.

They went together then, John with a giant straight scotch in his hand, back up to the attic. They pulled on the chain light above the attic steps, but no other.

The attic was very quiet. John's half-finished painting of feathers and shell sat against the easel. The white of empty canvases loomed out in the darkened room. Very gently the panes of the skylight and windows shook in the wind.

"She's not going to come now," John said, his voice low and angry.

"Shh," Willy said. "Don't be impatient. Let's wait."

They waited. Willy climbed the skylight steps and looked up, but saw nothing. She waited there a long while and still saw nothing. John sat on his high stool, looking out the window, but he saw only the harbor, dark except for the passing flicker of a ship's lights, and the sky, dark except for the random twinkling lights of a plane flying from Nantucket to Hyannis.

They waited perhaps an hour. They heard the wind rattling the windows and the sound of each other's breathing. Nothing else.

Finally they agreed to go back downstairs. John fixed himself another scotch; Willy fixed dinner. John sat at the dining-room table, letting his food grow cold, telling Willy over and over again every detail he could remember about the ghost.

When he was sipping his third scotch, Willy said, "The painting in the attic, John—the one of the shell and the berry and the feathers. That's what you're working on now, isn't it? It's very good, I think. And not like your usual work."

John smiled. "You like it? Good. It's painstaking work. I want to get the color and detail just right. I'm going to work on it tomorrow." He paused, then grimaced. "Ghost or no ghost, Willy, I'm going back to the attic to work on it tomorrow."

CHAPTER FOUR

THE NEXT MORNING, JOHN AWOKE FEELING HUNG OVER, EX-
hausted, and embarrassed. A *ghost.* He cringed at the remem-
brance of the evening before. He showered and shaved and
shook his head at himself in the mirror. "You lunatic," he said.

For his reasoning had returned. He knew there were no
such things as ghosts and realized now in the bright light of day
that what had happened last night had been only an illusion
brought on by his nerves and whatever light and shadows the
tossing trees had thrown against the skylight. Part of it came
from stress, probably. He had not told even Willy how much he
wanted to do something important with his art and how afraid
he was that he didn't have sufficient talent. He had read enough
psychology to know about the twists and tricks anxiety could
play on a person's mind. He vowed to be more sensible, less
panicked about his work. He was only beginning. He had five
years.

Willy sewed curtains for her sewing-room windows. She
had found a heavy chintz fabric, cream, covered with birds,

66

flowers, and fruits in colors of peach and rose and turquoise blue. She put down one of their smaller Oriental rugs in the room, the slate blue with ivory border, and by the end of the week her room was finished. She set out her favorite items on the built-in bookshelf: favorite books between porcelain bookends, photos of herself and John in malachite or silver frames, shells and rocks she had collected from the beach. Her stereo and records were in one corner, next to the small padded lady's chair she sometimes sat in to relieve her aching back when she embroidered for long hours. She had a mahogany cabinet filled with threads, fabrics, and needles and a long mahogany table covered with the different frames she used. She was ready to work on a new piece but hadn't decided what she wanted to do yet.

Feeling slightly guilty about devoting so much time to her own private room, she resolved to spend the next few weeks just on the house—and on Christmas. She loved Christmas. She brought boxes out of the storage room at the back of the house and took out the decorations they had used for eight years. She went into the village and bought a wreath, which she decorated herself with an enormous plaid bow and pinecones and red berries she found on the moors. She wove fresh greens into the frame that held four Advent candles and bought new purple Advent tapers at Robinson's Five and Ten. She arranged these along the mantel in the dining room and felt melancholy; this was their first Christmas away from Boston, and they would be lonely here, knowing no one.

Sunday morning she rose, dressed, and went off to church by herself, partly because she loved church, especially at Christmas, but partly from a need just to *see* other people. It was interesting to her that John, who ordinarily lived among crowds of friends and colleagues, was showing no signs of missing others around him and in fact seemed quite content with his new solitude. He was still sleeping when she returned at noon, and so she spent the next hour setting up the crèche on one of the living room end tables. She had made the crèche when she was thirteen and had sculpted the small pieces from clay and painted them herself, in brilliant colors. Her art teacher, who had doted on her, fired the pieces for her, and her parents had set these awkward, homely pieces in a place of honor on the marble mantel in their elegant living room. Now Willy set them up every Christmas and smiled to see her long-nosed Virgin Mary, her spindly Joseph, her lopsided and bucktoothed wise men.

Later, she and John read the Sunday papers, then took a long walk on the beach, wrapped up in wool scarves, hats, coats, and gloves. It was cold and windy; winter was coming on. They ate thick, juicy cheeseburgers at the Brotherhood and watched "Masterpiece Theater." Willy went to bed then with a book, because John, who hadn't worked all day, decided to go up to the attic to look over the painting he had just finished. He stayed there for an hour or so. When he returned, he was in a good humor, pleased with what he had accomplished that week, and he went downstairs to get them each a Courvoisier. They sat in bed like buddies, sipping their brandy and talking. There was no more mention of ghosts. A week had passed without any sign of the ghost, and while they had not forgotten the incident, it had faded in importance; soon it would be just a good story to tell.

ANOTHER WEEK PASSED, GHOST-FREE.

On Saturday morning, Willy nuzzled next to John as they lay stretching in their warm bed.

"Guess what," she said. "You're taking the day off. Don't argue. I haven't seen you all week, and I won't let you work today. This is worse than when you worked for the Blackstone Group. I want to go Christmas shopping today. I want to walk around town with you and look at the lights and the shops. Come on, sweetie, be a sport," she teased, running her hands over his body, touching him in persuasive places.

John thought about it. He had finished the last feather-and-shell painting yesterday; he was at a good stopping place. "Okay," he said. "I'm all yours today."

While he was shaving, he called Willy into the bathroom. "Look," he said, pointing to his mustache. He hadn't clipped it for a long time, and it was growing longer than he'd ever let it get before. "What would you think if I let it grow like this?" he asked, indicating with his hands how the mustache would droop down around the ends of his mouth.

"I think it would look good. . . ." Willy said, cocking her head to one side, considering. "Sort of old-fashioned, perhaps. But you have an old-fashioned face."

John studied his face in the mirror and silently agreed with Willy. He liked his looks; he knew he was handsome enough. His dark hair was still thick and waved directly back from his forehead and temples. He sometimes thought he was the only man on the East Coast who didn't part his hair on the left. This style suited him, showed off his broad brow, dark-lashed eyes, straight nose. He'd always had a mustache, but a well-groomed, clipped one. He thought now, eyeing himself in the mirror, that if he let it grow out longer, he'd look better, more romantic, more like an artist.

"You'd look like Jesse James." Willy laughed, watching him study himself. "You're so vain. Come on, gorgeous, the world is waiting."

He pulled on corduroy trousers, a plaid flannel shirt, and a crew-neck sweater, one that didn't have holes in it or paint on it like the ones he worked in. Willy was wearing gray tweed pants and a thick red pullover that showed off her bosom. She had stuck her hair into an elaborate twist.

"We're a fine pair!" John announced as he helped her into

her fur jacket. He threw a white silk scarf over his sheepskin coat and watched Willy pull on her purple leather gloves. He whistled as they went out the door, and they were both caught up in a holiday mood.

They spent the morning choosing their tree, bringing it in and getting it set up in the stand. They rewarded themselves with a long lunch at the Boardinghouse, with a bottle of good red wine and a rich chocolate dessert. It was two-thirty before they set out again to shop.

Willy wanted to buy Anne a shawl from Nantucket Looms; she wanted to look at baby blankets and baby clothes for presents for the Hunters. After an hour, John began to get restless. They agreed to part ways and to meet later for a drink. John went off intending to buy Willy something fabulous for Christmas.

But everywhere he went, he was ambushed by art galleries. He had known there were a lot in Nantucket; that was one of the attractions for him. But he had never spent any time in them, and now, in spite of his best intentions, he found himself lured inside. He ended up spending the afternoon studying the artwork in every gallery he could find.

So much of it was good. So much of it was very good. There was a great variety, from superrealism to abstract, from modern impressionist pieces that danced with light to modern primitivism. He paid little attention to the photography or sculptures or woven pieces or to the "sailor's valentines," the intricate designs made from hundreds of tiny shells glued together in elaborate arrangements. Only the watercolors, sketches, and oils interested him, and by the end of the afternoon he realized that he had been looking at all the artwork from the viewpoint of a competitor.

And he had to admit to himself that compared with what he saw here, he was not very good. In his mind's eye he compared his paintings of feathers and shell and knew they were lacking. They were heavy-handed, rigid, stark—soulless. They were merely *tours de force.*

The main street of Nantucket was elaborately decorated for Christmas. Not only did each small shop have a charming scene or arrangement of lights in its windows; real Christmas trees had been placed on the sidewalks in front of each shop. At least thirty trees adorned Main Street, each decorated by various grades at the local elementary school or by the Girl or Boy Scouts or by church groups, so that some trees were hung with the bright flags of different countries or with handmade dioramas of Christmas scenes or with gold bows or seashells or dolls. Now, at dusk, colored lights were switched on all these small trees as well as on the long strand that looped and swirled all around a towering tree at the bottom of Main Street.

John walked down the gaily lighted brick sidewalks, crossed the cobblestone streets, oblivious to the charm of the town. Hands stuffed into his coat pockets, he responded with a gruff grunt when excited Christmas shoppers accidentally brushed against his shoulder in passing. The world didn't need another artist, he told himself; certainly didn't need a half-assed one. He was a fool.

Over hot-buttered rum at the Tap Room, Willy tried to console him.

"Patience, John," she said. "You've only just begun. And how do you know you're not good? No one else has seen the work yet."

She continued this way for a while. But John had grown sullen on this crisp winter day, and after an hour of trying to cheer him up, Willy gave up. They walked down darkened Orange Street to their house side by side but not speaking. Back in the house, Willy didn't even begin to suggest that they try to decorate their tree. She informed John that she wasn't very hungry and would spend the evening with a mystery and a giant bowl of popcorn.

John told Willy that was fine with him; he wasn't hungry, either. He was going to go back up to the attic. He knew he was bad company, but he couldn't shake his mood. So Willy curled up on the sofa with an afghan over her knees, a great bowl of salted popcorn in her lap, and her paperback mystery in her hand. She left him for another world.

John turned on only the stairwell light in the attic. He didn't want to see too clearly. He stood in the gloom by the broken humidifier, picking up the feathers and watching them fall back to the surface. Even separated from the bird they adorned, they kept the spirit of the bird intact; they did not simply plummet but rather wafted with a gentle lilting movement, gracefully downward, landing without the slightest sound. Such easy, obvious beauty; why couldn't he capture it? What kind of man was he to drag his wife here, to live off her money, in order to turn out mediocrity? He picked up the small, shriveled rose hip, wanting to crush it in his hand, but it was so small it only settled in the hollow of his palm.

A gentle knocking came at the skylight.

"Great," John said sardonically. "Now I get the ghost again."

He had had four drinks at the Tap Room, and while he was not drunk, he was in a bad enough and stewed enough mood to feel for one bitter moment that this ghost business was just another personal jibe from fate. He felt belligerent and tromped over to the steps to the skylight without any kind of fear at all.

But fear struck through him, sobering him completely, when he climbed partway up the steps and saw the woman there, just outside the skylight, just as she had been before. Young, troubled, beautiful, beseeching—a pale woman with streaming dark hair and a heavy dark cape leaned over the skylight, beating against the glass with her small hands.

It frightened him that she was there. But she was not in herself a frightening sight. She was so small and so pretty, and the look on her face indicated that he was the one with the power.

John forced himself to look at the woman, not to look away. He was shaking so hard with fear that his whole body reverberated against the wooden steps, making small hitting noises, and his heart thudded loudly in his chest and ears. She was there. She was there. He was not mad. She was really there.

"Fuck," John whispered. "Jesus."

Now that the woman saw that John was looking at her steadily, she stopped battering the panes with her hands and leaned down close to the glass of the skylight. Some of her dark hair fell over the side of her face; he could see the wavy sheen of it, the lustrous texture of it, as clearly as he could see the grain in the wooden steps.

Her mouth was half open, as if she meant to speak. Her eyes were the eyes of a real woman: dark and wide and luminous, filled with a message.

"Let me in," she called. "Please. Let me in."

He heard her clearly. Her voice was like music.

He thought, Well, this will prove something one way or the other, before he said aloud, "All right. Stand back."

John backed down the steps, grabbed up some rags he used to wipe his brushes, and wrapped them around his hand. Then he climbed back up the steps. The ghost was still there. She had moved back, just slightly, so that he could still see her.

He raised his arm and drove his fist upward through the skylight, smashing it so that the glass shattered and fell in fragments and shards all around him. Much of it stayed anchored in the frame, so that the center, where he had struck the blow, was now a jagged hole and the chilly winter night air whooshed in through this hole, passing over his body so suddenly that it was as if he had plunged headfirst into a swimming pool; he had the sensation of falling, of being surrounded by cold, and he lost his breath with the shock.

73

The woman was no longer there. He heard a tinkle as one last splinter of glass hit the wooden floor. He felt the cold air blowing evenly now through the broken glass, hitting him in the face. He stared, he waited, but the woman did not return.

"Fuck," he said under his breath.

He backed down the leaning steps, unwrapping the rag. In spite of that precaution, one knuckle was bleeding, and his whole hand ached from the impact. He stood at the bottom of the steps and carefully picked pieces of glass from his hair. The temperature was falling rapidly now in the attic, and the floor around the steps was a dangerous mess of glittering broken glass.

"Intelligent, John," he said to himself. "Fucking brilliant."

It wouldn't do to let the wind and damp get into the attic. Even if what he had done was worthless, there were still all the new canvases. He ripped a heavy moving box so that he had a section of cardboard suitable to cover the hole and found a roll of masking tape with his other supplies. He climbed back up the ladder and covered the skylight with the cardboard, taping it tightly to the wooden frame. It pulsed slightly from the beat of the wind but did not give. He would have to get a carpenter here as soon as possible.

And tell him what? And tell Willy what? Christ, he was a fool. If only that—if only he weren't losing his mind.

He backed down the steps again and stood looking at the sparkling glass that glinted from the floor. That could wait until tomorrow to be cleaned up. He'd have to bring the vacuum up to get every tiny bit of it.

A movement, a shadow passing, startled him, and he looked up. The young woman in the black cape was standing at the top of the stairs leading down to the second floor. She had loosened her cape slightly so that he could see the gray worsted stuff of her dress, which fell in folds to her feet. Now that she was inside, there was color to her: Her lips and cheeks were a tender pink. But her eyes and hair were still black, and her skin very white.

Again John's heart started up its drumming against his chest. His mouth went dry. He was too alarmed to speak, even though he opened his mouth. He felt frozen in his terror, as if he were in one of his most awful nightmares, where he could not move.

"Thank you," the woman said sweetly, simply. She smiled. "For letting me in."

She turned and went down the steps to the second floor. He heard the latch being lifted on the door between the attic steps and the second floor, but he could tell from the way the light did not change that the door had not opened. Yet when he managed to move forward a few feet to stare down the stairway, he saw that the woman had gone.

"Dammit!" he yelled. "Where did you go?"

He thundered down the wooden steps and opened the door himself—the handle was not a new round one but rather a wrought-iron latch contraption that had to be lifted up and out of a little iron notch.

On the second floor the hall was empty. John ran from room to room, looking, finding nothing. He opened the closets.

Nothing.

He ran back up to scan the attic.

No one. Nothing.

He ran down the stairs to the first floor and looked through all the rooms and all the closets and cupboards in all the rooms.

He heard footsteps and turned, gasping.

"What on earth is the matter, John?" Willy asked, coming up to him as he stood nearly panting in the front hall. "My God, look at you."

For his hair was wild, hanging in his eyes, and one hand was bruised and clotted with blood.

"She's here," John said. "She's inside. I let her in."

Willy looked at her husband, and the worry on her face only enraged him. "Who's here, John?" she asked gently.

"The ghost, dammit!" John yelled. "Willy, you've got to believe me. I bashed open the skylight. I let her in. I saw her on the attic staircase. I heard her speak. And then she went down to the second floor and went through the door—and disappeared. She's somewhere in the house, and I can't find her. Dammit, Willy, I'm telling you the truth." He was nearly sobbing with fear and frustration.

"I believe you, John," Willy said quietly. "I believe you. Do you want me to look for her with you?"

"Yes," he said.

So they went through the house together, slowly, but found nothing. They found no one and no sign of anyone, no sign that anyone else had been in the house. In the attic, the cardboard John had taped to the skylight pulsed gently with the wind.

"Christ, Willy," John said, leaning against the wall. "I'm scared. I'm really scared." He managed a grin. "I'm more scared now that she *isn't* here than I was when she was. I don't want you to think I'm . . . going mad or something. Jesus."

"I don't think that," Willy said. "I promise you, John. I don't think that. Let's go to bed now. Come on."

"Bed?" John said, as if the thought were foreign. "Willy, I won't be able to sleep."

"No, probably not," Willy said. "But it's so late now. We can just sit in bed and talk. Relax. I'll get us some brandies."

Willy and John sat together in their bed, leaning against the pillows they had propped against the headboard, and the air of the room was gently steady and brightened by their bedside lamps. John felt safe inside the light's protection, in the way a child feels safe.

He described the scene again to Willy, carefully providing every detail he could remember. He had heard her voice.

Several times. Had seen the material of her dress so clearly that he could tell it was scratchy, heavy, weighted. Had seen her face so clearly that he could tell her skin was creamy and that her cheeks were flushed rosy with fear or excitement or—or something.

"She was very beautiful," John confided, embarrassed by this detail.

"Well, at least there's that." Willy smiled. "At least she's not some creaking skeleton clanking chains around. Or some old ghoul. It could be worse."

"Tell me what you think, Willy. What you really think about this."

Willy sipped her brandy, pulled her knees up to her chest, and wrapped her arms around them. She was wearing a pair of John's pajamas, striped red and white; she wore these when she was in her period or sick and wanted to be sloppy and comfortable. Now the sight of Willy in them was somehow comforting to John. She looked sensible. Comradely.

"Here's what I think," she said slowly. "The truth. It's one of two things, I think. Either it's a trick of your mind—now wait a minute, let me finish! A trick of your mind. Because you've sort of gone cold turkey on people, you know. For years you saw hordes of people every day, and now you see only me, and for the past few days you've spent more time alone than with me or anyone else. Maybe it's like a mirage, like someone crawling through a desert dying of thirst, seeing a pool of water in the distance. It could be something like that, John."

She could tell John was not happy with this explanation. "Or," she went on, "it could be a ghost. I didn't really believe in them, and you didn't, either, but we could have been wrong. I mean, why would people talk about ghosts for centuries if there wasn't some kind of truth to it? And this is an old house. People say that old houses do have ghosts. It probably really is a ghost—and that's sort of neat, don't you think? I mean, as I said, it seems like a nice kind of ghost, a pretty woman instead of some creepy old thing that wakes us in the night with hideous laughter. Maybe it's some woman who used to live here. Anyway, if it's a ghost, I'm bound to see her sometime, too. Then you'll know you're not nuts."

John looked at his wife. Her hair was unbraided and fell, thick as honey, all around her face and shoulders and arms. "Do you have any idea how much I love you?" he asked.

Willy smiled. She set her brandy on the bedside table and scooted over to wiggle herself inside his arms. "Umm," she said.

". . . how much I need you," John said, almost whispering.

"I think I know what will help you fall asleep," Willy said.

And a while later, she proved right.

~~~~~~~

WILLY WAS SENSIBLE. SHE HAD ASSUMED FROM THE START THAT during their marriage she and John would have to endure crises. Perhaps work, or in-laws, although John had none, because her family was all dead, and she liked his family very much. She assumed they would have their share of arguments over children, when to have them, how to raise them, over all the decisions of a shared life. She had never expected their lives to be perfect. She had always known she would have to face problems. But she had not counted on something like this—a ghost. Who would plan for that?

Willy had even gone so far in her mind as to admit to herself that perhaps there would come a time when John or she would feel drawn to another person. She could imagine it, oh, sometime far in the future, when John turned fifty, for example, or when she was overcome with the frantic practicalities of raising a family, for she had seen such things happen to friends. She had imagined that one or both of them at some time might become infatuated with someone else, and she had known she could endure this, too. Because she was so certain that she and John would never separate. They loved each other too much.

78

She did not think either of them would actually be unfaithful to the other; they weren't the type. But they might *want* to be unfaithful someday—that was what she had thought could happen—and had planned on dealing with that, too. Then they would go away, for a long vacation. They were lucky enough to have the money for such things. Or they would do something drastic—move, have a child, spend a year in Europe, build a house, take up judo together, something, she couldn't know so far in advance just what—that would prevent any danger to their marriage, that would end the infatuation.

But she would have staked her life—in a way, *was* staking her life—on the belief that she and John would always stay together. They had been so lucky to find each other. They needed each other so much. Their desires and likes and dislikes and needs and eccentricities all fit together so well, and at the foundation of it all was the irrational, furious, magical, sexual, endless electricity of love and lust that had drawn them together and continually surged through and around them, keeping them together, keeping them alive. They truly had found—or had been found by—that thing in the universe that was so rare and so huge, that made their sum more than the total of their parts.

Some nights they lay in bed just kissing, kissing each other all over, Willy kissing John's torso from his nipples down along the swirl of hair that led to his belly button, to his genitals, burying her face between his thighs, kissing him there, her long hair sliding over his chest and abdomen, while his back arched slightly in pleasure. Or John kissing Willy on her mouth, her face, her neck, her shoulders, her arms and hands and breasts, while she said his name, said wild things, wild nighttime words of desire and praise. It was more than sex; it was a communion of joy in their mutual existence, an amazed expression of their love.

Willy loved John passionately, and sensibly. But the week after he saw the ghost was hard on her love in ways she'd never dreamed of. John kept seeing the ghost, and Willy never did. And the things John said the ghost did were so very strange.

Every morning John claimed that he had been awakened in the night by the ghost, always the same ghost, the woman. The first three nights, it was only that he awakened from his sleep to find her bending over him, studying his face. He said she had been smiling when he awakened; he could see her smile by the dim light of the room, and when he opened his eyes, she waited until he focused on her, until their eyes met, and that connection was made when two people silently acknowledge the other's presence. Then, she had vanished. Just vanished, into the air. Now you see her, now you don't, just like that.

The next two nights, John said, he had awakened from his sleep not only to see her, but to *feel* her. He felt her hand caressing his face, like a mother caressing a sleeping child, he said. The ghost, leaning over him, had softly drawn her small hand across his brow and down the side of his face. Like someone blind reading braille. She had also lightly, slowly, drawn her fingertips over his mouth. Lingered there. Then vanished. With trembling fingers John had retraced the places on his face where the ghost had touched him.

Now, this morning, John sat at the kitchen table in the clear morning sunlight and looked at Willy and said that last night the ghost had kissed him.

First she had bent over, looking at him; then she had caressed his face with her hand; and then, smiling, she had come closer to him, her long dark hair falling over her shoulders to brush against his face. She had kissed him lightly, sweetly, but firmly.

"Her hair smells so sweet, Willy, like apples, like new-mown grass in the spring—the fragrance is so powerful I can't believe you don't smell it, too!" John said.

"Was her mouth opened or closed?" Willy asked, surprising herself by the question.

"Open. Slightly." John looked away, embarrassed. "I mean her tongue was not in my mouth, if that's what you want to know," he said, looking back at Willy, almost angry. "But I could feel her lips. I could feel her breath." He stared at Willy defiantly.

Willy turned her face away. The morning was brilliant, with a cold sun brightening the room. Her coffee, strong and hot and sweet, sat before them on the wooden table. Her husband sat across from her, telling her he had been kissed by another woman. By a ghost.

"Willy," John said. "Please."

Willy looked up at her husband, and her strength returned. "I have an idea," she said.

So they sat together, making their plan.

THAT NIGHT, WILLY HAD A LOVELY DREAM. SHE WAS WARM, BUT A sweet cool breeze was blowing against the curtains in her sewing room, and the birds and flowers were coming alive. The bluebirds lifted off the chintz material, carrying the fruits— plums, cherries, tight green pears—in their mouths. They flew about the room and landed on the flowers, which had also come alive from the curtains and grew in elaborate, fragrant twists and arches against the wall. How beautiful the world could be! Willy thought as she dreamed, and felt something pinch her.

She was puzzled. Her mind quickly separated itself into two parts: one part keeping her under just enough to save the dream, the other struggling toward consciousness, alert, alarmed. For a second, her fantasy lapped over into reality, and she dreamed that a bird had nipped her, a thorn from the flowers had pricked her. But finally she came awake and realized that she was lying in their dark bedroom, snuggled under covers.

81

John was pinching the skin of her thigh so hard it stung.

She looked in his direction. He was awake, staring upward. He kept pinching Willy.

She remembered: this was the plan they had agreed on. When John was awakened again by the ghost, he would touch Willy with his hand, hidden under the covers, covertly awakening her. Willy did not move, but she came completely awake. Without moving, she carefully looked around the room. Enough light shone in through the curtains from the street lamps so that she could see the furniture and the pictures on the walls clearly. She saw nothing unusual.

John kept pinching her.

"Stop it, John. It hurts!" she hissed, her voice barely audible.

But at the sound of her voice, John raised up in bed, turned toward Willy on one elbow. He was smiling, triumphant.

"There!" John said. "You saw her *then,* didn't you?"

Willy stared at her husband. For a split second she was tempted to lie, but she had already given herself away. Even in the darkened room, John could read her expression.

"Shit!" John said, and raised his fist and brought it down in such a violent gesture that Willy flinched back, thinking he meant to hit her. But he only pounded the pillow. "I can't believe you didn't see her, Willy. She was *right there.* Standing by the bed, next to me, bending over me, looking at me. Christ, her hair was touching the blankets. She was kissing my face, Willy! *Christ,* I can't believe you didn't see her! Did you look? Did you look hard? Where I told you to look? She vanished the instant you spoke. Did you forget our plan? Did you speak before you looked for her?"

"I looked, John," Willy said. "I looked very carefully. I was absolutely wide awake—how could I not be with you pinching me so hard?—I looked all around the room without moving anything but my eyes."

"And you saw nothing? Absolutely nothing?"

"Nothing."

"Well, fuck!" John said. "Just fuck!" He flung himself from their bed and switched on a bedside lamp, nearly knocking it over in his fury. He stormed around the room, ranging from bed to window to bureau and back again to bed, his fists clenched at his sides. "Fuck," he said, "this is just unbelievable. This is just unendurable."

Willy took John's pillow and propped it on her own, then scooted up against them both so that she could watch her husband in his agitation. She pulled the covers to her chin. She felt both sympathy for and irritation at John. And a kind of fear. She had never seen him like this before.

"She's got some nerve, I'll say that for her," Willy said, speaking her feelings aloud. John turned in his pacing, stopped, to look at his wife. "I mean, what a brazen hussy she must be, to come in and kiss you while you're lying in bed with your wife. John, I don't think your ghost has very good morals."

"Dammit, Willy, don't joke about this!" John exploded, losing his fear in a fury at his wife. "This is not a fucking joke!"

"Well, what do you want me to do?" Willy yelled back. "I didn't see her! I *can't* see her. I've never seen her. Yet you tell me some woman I can't see is coming in at night and kissing you while we're in bed? What do you expect me to do? What do you want me to do?"

They glared at each other, stalemated.

"Come back to bed," Willy said at last, relenting. She put John's pillow back in its place and smoothed the rumpled covers and patted his place by her side. "Please. Come back to bed. We'll talk about it in the morning when we're not so tired. It will be easier to deal with by daylight, I think. Come on, John."

Reluctantly, John crawled back into bed. He turned off the light. He and Willy lay holding each other for a while, silently making up for their moment of anger. Then John turned over so they lay like spoons, but apart, and Willy ran her hand over her husband's back. The touching relaxed them both. Their bed was warm, and it was after four in the morning. Willy felt her eyes closing, could feel sleep rising with its seductive comfort, blanketing her consciousness. But she sensed John lying next to her, still awake.

"It's all right," she said finally, longing for sleep. "She has never come twice in the same night, John. She won't come again. You can sleep."

And at last he slept.

THE NEXT MORNING, THEY AWAKENED TO RAIN AND WIND; IT WAS snowing on the mainland, but here the storm brought only rain. When Willy went out to get groceries, she took a drive past the Coast Guard station at Brant Point. Through the streaming rain she saw, flying high on the masts, the red triangular gale-force-wind flags—flags of warning.

Willy hurried back to her house. She wanted to sit down with John and talk for a long time about the ghost, leaving nothing out, planning some kind of defense against it, whether it was hallucination or real. The flags had made danger seem possible.

But when she entered the kitchen, she found Kirk Beauregard there, talking to John. The wind and rain had driven the workers indoors.

Kirk showed Willy and John the sketches he'd made for building bookshelves in the front room so they could turn it into a library. That was his first project, he said, which would take only about a week, and then a few days more for his men to stain the shelves. Then he went up to the attic with John to take measurements for a new pane of glass for the skylight window.

John said he'd heard noises on the roof, thought it was birds or creatures trapped there, had been hitting at the ceiling with a broomstick, and had accidentally broken the skylight.

The carpenter didn't seem surprised, disbelieving, or even particularly interested. He recommended using plexiglas to replace the glass and went off to Marine Lumber to get it. The electrician showed up, such a large, lumbering man that it was hard to believe he could handle delicate wires, and began to run another line of electricity up to the attic so that John could have more power there. So men came in and out of the house all day, and there was no time when Willy and John could talk at length alone.

They did speak about the ghost, in a cautious, joking sort of way, with Kirk when he sat down with them in the late morning for a cup of coffee.

"You know," John said, smiling, "my wife and I are beginning to think we've got a ghost in the house."

"Wouldn't be surprised," Kirk said. "A lot of these old Nantucket houses have ghosts." He proceeded to tell them tales of footsteps, rustlings, sighings, lifted latches, of workers who got spooked and wouldn't work in certain houses.

"But have *you* ever seen one of the ghosts?" John asked, intent now. "Ever spoken to one of them? Or known anyone who has?"

Kirk Beauregard grinned at John. "No, I can't say I have," he replied, letting John know with his smile that he might enjoy a good story, but he didn't take any of it seriously.

That night was a good television night, and Willy and John ate their lasagna and salads and fruit in the living room, watching the news and an HBO movie. They had spent the day dealing with the myriad decisions about the house, and by bedtime they were too tired to start up any serious discussion about the ghost.

As they went upstairs to bed, though, John said, "Willy, I

think I'll sleep in the guest room tonight. Maybe—maybe she won't bother me there."

And Willy was so glad to hear that the ghost was a bother to him, that in spite of the fact that she was beautiful and had kissed him, John wasn't eager to see her, that she turned on the stairs and with a big rush of love put her arms on John's shoulders.

"Oh, no, please," she said. "There are twin beds in the guest room. I couldn't lie next to you. And I don't want you so far away from me, in another room. I don't sleep well when we're not together—and you don't either. Look, let's trade sides of the bed. You sleep on my side, I'll sleep on yours. Then maybe, if the ghost comes, I'll see her. Maybe we'll trick her."

John smiled up at his wife; standing on the stairs as they were, she rose slightly above him, and he buried his head against her breasts, nuzzling into her. Just so easily, so quickly, the distance, the formality that had been between them all day, vanished.

"All right," he said. "Let's do that."

Lying in bed in their switched places, waiting for sleep and what the night might bring, they both felt uneasy and restless. So they curled toward each other and lay talking for a long time.

They told bedtime stories. Willy told John about the family reunion she had gone to long ago when she had members of her family still alive. There had been a lot of them, mostly very old people, and she had been the only child. Because the house where they converged didn't have enough bedrooms for everyone, she had been forced to sleep with her father's great-aunt. At the time, Willy was seven; the great-aunt was a formidable ninety-one but she had a huge eiderdown bed and said she'd love to have Willy with her for the night. It was scary enough sleeping in a strange room in a large, dark, shadowy old house; even worse sleeping in the vast feather bed that seemed to pull Willy down in a smothering embrace next to a woman so old and wrinkled and skeletal. Once settled in bed, the great-aunt immediately fell asleep, her breath regular and as rasping as a saw. Willy was afraid the old crone would die right next to her, and so she lay awake all night, terrified, listening to the loud ticking of the walnut clock on the bedroom mantel, and to the wheezing, snorting, gargling, rasping sounds the old woman made in her sleep.

John told Willy about the night he had camped out with his scout troop the year he was eleven. Each tent held two people; the scoutmaster made them draw tentmate names out of a hat. John had drawn Martin Sylvester, a boy all the other boys suspected of being a fairy. Resigned, John had unrolled his sleeping bag as close to the side of the tent as he could get and had faked sleep immediately so he wouldn't have to get involved in even a private conversation with the weirdo. It had been awful lying there on the hard ground, hearing the stifled giggles and whispers of his friends in the tents all around him. But at last he had fallen asleep, only to awaken at some point in the night to feel something pressing against his thigh. The awful Martin, he thought, and had moved away, inching even closer to his side of the tent. The pressing continued, a live, warm nudging; John, enraged and ever prepared, grabbed the Boy Scout flashlight that he had placed near his head and in one wild movement turned over, flashed on the light, and yelled, "God damn it, Martin, leave me alone!" And had seen a long black snake that had come in to shelter against him from the cold go slithering peacefully out of the tent, back into the night. He had been razzed about that for months.

Willy and John snuggled close, talking and laughing, and the night darkened around them, friendly and normal, just another night. At last they turned over, facing away from each other, and fell asleep, hips touching; it was comforting, falling asleep this way.

In the middle of the night Willy's dreams became confused, and she dreamed at first that she was a doll, a baby, being fussed over and undressed.

She came awake at once when John thrust his penis inside her, hurting her. She had been sound asleep; she was not ready for him.

"John," she said, "hey."

She tried to push him away, to slow him down, for he was pounding against her. He had pushed her flannel nightgown up around her arms and somehow gotten her underpants off; she could feel them hanging around one ankle.

"John," she said again. This is like being raped, she thought, for he was smashing his mouth against hers, holding her arms down with his hands, and thrusting into her heavily, as if he were battering his way into a room.

"God damn it, John, stop it!" Willy cried at last, and tried to shove him away, but he came then and fell against her in a heap.

Willy lay with her head turned away from her husband, gasping for breath. She felt him subsiding against her. Then he rolled off of her onto his back, groaning.

"What on earth was that all about?" Willy asked.

"What do you mean?" John asked.

"I mean what you just did!" Willy said angrily. "That wasn't very nice, John. You've never done anything like it before."

"Well, you shouldn't have started it if you didn't want it," John said.

"What? What do you mean I shouldn't have started it? What are you talking about?" Willy raised up on one elbow to look at him.

"Christ, Willy, I'm talking about the way you were touching me," John said. "You've never done that before, either. You woke me from a deep sleep. Not that I didn't enjoy it," he added in a smug tone, reaching out to put his hand on Willy's hip.

"John," Willy said, pulling away from his hand, "I didn't touch you. I was asleep, and suddenly you were on top of me.

Couldn't you tell I wasn't ready for you? Couldn't you tell I was asleep?"

John took his hand away. Willy could feel how quiet he had gone.

"Now, Willy," he said at last, determined, raising up on his elbow to face Willy in the dark, "I felt you. I felt you wake me up. You were touching me. Kissing me . . . *fondling* me. God, don't you think I know what I felt? It wasn't any dream, I can tell you for sure. I wouldn't have pounced on you if you hadn't been arousing me like that."

Willy stared at her husband. "John," she said carefully, "believe me. I promise you. I swear to you. I was not touching you. Not kissing you. I was sleeping. I was sound asleep."

They stared at each other.

"Shit," John said under his breath, and punched his pillow. He turned over, facing away from Willy, and lay staring into the dark.

Willy lay flat on her back, rigid, also staring, wide-eyed, at the darkened room.

They did not speak. They lay together, side by side, afraid to speak, afraid to take their thoughts to the logical, and unbelievable, conclusion.

Willy began to cry. She was very quiet about it, stifling her sobs, letting the tears roll down her face onto the pillow, into her hair. John could feel her crying. Finally, he turned over and put his arm around her.

"It must have been a dream, Willy," he said. "One of those supervivid dreams."

They needed the lie to make them feel safe.

CHAPTER FIVE

T
HE MIND IS A STRANGE THING," GEORGE GLIDDEN SAID. "I'VE
seen patients who swore they had lunch with Jesus Christ."

John twisted uncomfortably in his chair and took another large swallow of white wine. He didn't care much for white wine, but he wanted the dulling effect of the alcohol. Willy looked across the table at him, steadily, trying to send him waves of sympathy.

They were at the Hunters' apartment in Boston, where Willy had insisted they spend Christmas, because after the night John had awakened her so violently, she was determined that they get away for a while, take a break from the house.

The ghost, fortunately, had not followed them, and for the past three nights they had slept peacefully all through the night in the Hunters' guest bedroom.

Willy did not think they had been mistaken in confiding their problem to Mark and Anne. The mistake had been in letting Mark bring it up now, at their dinner party. It was a small party, just the six of them, the Hunters, the Constables, and

George and Diana Glidden. Diana was all right, wonderful, really, pleasant and smart. And George was smart, too, but a terrible know-it-all. Mark probably had had only the best intentions in bringing the ghost business up with George, who was, after all, a very successful psychiatrist. But George wasn't going to let the subject drop. He never did when he could get his hands on any topic that he knew more about than most people. He loved the sound of his voice. He loved appearing to be wise. But if he really had been wise, he would have realized from John's expression that he should shut up.

"Now this ghost business," George went on, "is definitely in your mind. Absolutely. I mean, we're all intelligent people here, let's just agree from the start that we're going to look at it from an enlightened point of view. This is not the Middle Ages. We know now the sort of games the mind can play. We know why the mind plays them. Anxiety, stress, self-defense against knowledge too difficult to bear. . . . However, in *your* case, John, I'd say the cause is different, and really much more interesting. Fascinating, really."

What could they all do then but look toward George with bated breath so he could give them the answer? And perhaps, Willy thought hopefully, perhaps he really does have the answer.

"You're an artist," George went on. "You have the soul of the artist, the mind of the artist, the desires of the artist. You read poetry, you will admit that poetry is as much a part of your mental makeup as, say, football might be of the average man's. Right?"

John nodded agreement.

"Now," George went on, "you come to a crisis in your life. You have put it all on the line, everything. You've decided to act like an artist, to work at your art. You've left your job, your friends, your hometown. You've gone off to an island and isolated yourself, you've put everything you've got into this

91

decision, this desire . . . this *obsession,* if I may. Let's say that secretly you're worried, a little anxious about this decision. Let's say you're feeling a little alone against the world now . . . not even Willy can help you in this situation. It's all up to you to prove yourself as an artist. Your self-esteem, your self-image, perhaps even the *meaning of your life,* depend on whether or not you make it as an artist.

"A lot of stress for the mind to take. A pretty heavy task for a man to bear alone. So what does your subconscious do for you to help you out during this time? You're a literate, well-read man. . . . Your subconscious pulls an idea out of the vast well of knowledge hidden in your mind and presents you with—*a muse.*"

George leaned back in his chair, triumphant. He smiled. Took a large sip of wine. Lit a cigarette.

Anne was too fascinated even to think of clearing off the dessert plates or suggesting that they move into the living room for coffee.

"George," she said, "what a marvelous idea."

George nodded, agreeing. "It all fits, you see. This is why the 'ghost' is female. Young. Beautiful. It's why Willy never sees her. Why she came to the attic *where John works.* Why she came, as it were, not from inside the house but from the heavens. Why she visits you at night, the time when the subconscious is filling up with creative power. Remember when you first saw her? You said you were drawing seaweed streaming like hair. Then you drew her—*then* she appeared in the window. She is a figment of your imagination, John. You have invented her because you need her."

John looked at Willy. He had not told the Hunters everything; he had said only that the ghost leaned over him at the bedside. They had not told them about the times she had kissed John or touched him intimately.

"My guess is," George went on, "that she'll continue to appear to you as long as you have any anxiety about your work.

At least until you get settled into it and believe that what you're doing has some kind of merit. It's too much to take on alone. You're really very clever, don't you see? You've provided yourself with a muse to inspire you."

"And your advice is . . ." Anne prompted.

"To go with it. Relax. Accept her. Don't be afraid of her. Let her into your life, into your mind, and I wouldn't be surprised at all if the creative juices didn't start to flow for you. But don't fight it. Don't try to pretend she doesn't appear or be angry when she does. I think your mind is doing this in order to help you, John. Your 'ghost' is on your side."

There was complete silence in the room. Mark broke it, saying, "Listen, George, do you think you could arrange for me to have one of those? Do a little hypnosis with me and get me a little gorgeous, nubile nighttime visitor that my wife couldn't see? God, John, I think you've really tapped into something marketable here. I mean, a pretty woman who comes into your bedroom but your wife can't see her?"

"You're going to get it later," Anne threatened, and everyone laughed and the tension broke. People rose, pushed their chairs back, went into the living room. Anne asked about coffee, tea, and the conversation turned to other things.

Willy watched John, who seemed more at ease now, perhaps because he was engaged in a conversation with Diana, who was nice, or perhaps, Willy thought, Willy hoped, because George Glidden, for all his pomposity, had somehow helped John. And George was smart, a fine psychiatrist—he could be right. He really could be right. The creative mind *was* an odd thing. She had wondered before what she would have thought if Pablo Picasso had been her husband and had wandered in with one of his abstracts; would she have thought to praise him, or would she have called the doctor?

Anne served the coffee and brandies, then sank down on the sofa next to Willy.

"Old times," she said. "Lovely having you two here." She

leaned closer, said sotto voce, "And we can gossip about them when they've gone."

Willy smiled back, a conspirator's smile, but she didn't feel it in her heart. There was a distance now between her and Anne. First of all, Anne talked about little else but the baby that was due in a month; she went on and on about how it kicked, about labor and childbirth tales she had heard and names she and Mark were deciding on.

It seemed to Willy that Anne had talked of nothing else these past three days. Yet Anne meant to be close; she told Willy the most intimate details about her body changes and her sex life now with Mark. It was Willy who had drawn back and caused the distance, really. She did not feel comfortable talking about John's "ghost" with Anne, for one thing; she had not yet been able to decide just how she felt about it.

Actually she was frightened—and jealous, and angry. And then she and John had agreed not to tell anyone about that final night when he felt someone fondling him. They had tacitly agreed not to discuss it with each other, either; it was just too difficult to discuss—and what could they say? That it was bizarre? They both knew that. There were no precedents they could follow in dealing with this, no how-to books on the subject. They were just muddling along, hoping that it would all go away—hoping the ghost would go away and leave them alone with their lives.

But now Willy thought: It was possible that George Glidden was right. It was possible that John, in his great desire to develop his art, had put himself under the sort of mental stress that would make him create a muse, need a muse. Willy didn't pretend to understand how the mind worked, especially the artistic mind. She wasn't an artist, and yet there were times when she needed to be alone, when she needed her solitude and whatever daydreams floated through her mind as she embroidered. She could not have worked in the presence of company. Perhaps it was the same sort of thing for John, taken to an extreme degree. He needed his solitude and the visions that his creative energies provided him.

Willy decided to try to relax about it all. To believe that somehow George Glidden's theory was on the right track. To let John have his muse, his "ghost," and not to mind. After all, if this vision, this muse, this *thing*, whatever she was, from wherever she had been called forth, helped John in his art, she would be valuable; she would help John be happy, and in the long run, she would help Willy and John in their marriage.

THE NEXT EVENING, AS THEY DROVE TO HYANNIS TO TAKE THE CAR ferry back to Nantucket, Willy said some of these things to John. She told him that perhaps George Glidden had been right; that perhaps they shouldn't fight the "ghost" or be afraid of her, but rather let her into their lives.

"Let's see what happens," she said.

John had been quiet, listening to Willy. "George is such an ass," he said.

"I know," Willy agreed. "But he's not stupid. He knows a lot. And what better explanation can you provide for the presence of your ghost? I prefer it to anything else I can think of."

John took a deep breath, holding down anger. "All right," he said at last. "All right. *Fine.* That's *fine* with me. Let's leave it at that, can we? I'm sick of it."

He felt his wife's gaze on him then, felt her worry and compassion directed toward him, even sensed how she was now searching for the right words to say to him, how she was working on it rather than just speaking naturally. So before she could go on, he said more gently, "Please, Willy. Let's leave it alone." He looked over at her, forcing himself to smile for her.

"Let's talk about something else in the world," he said. "I think we've beaten this topic to death."

Willy reached over and stroked John's hair briefly. "Sweetie," she said. Then—and Thank God! John thought—she yawned and removed her hand and leaned against the car door. "I'm going to take a little nap if you don't mind," she said. "All those late nights . . ."

"Go ahead," John said. "We've got a good forty-five more minutes before we reach Hyannis."

When she was asleep, John's relief was enormous. It had been hard to keep from unfairly directing his anger at Willy; it had been a strain all during this "vacation." It was not really Willy's fault, or if it was, she had only meant well, had only meant to be helpful. Still, he felt violated. Betrayed. Insulted. To have that egomaniac George Glidden analyzing what was deepest and dearest to him had been infuriating. Even to have the man possess that knowledge was horrible. It had been hard enough to let Willy, and then Mark, and then his colleagues at the agency know that he wanted to be an artist, a *real* artist. They were his friends; he could trust them, and if he failed, they would not laugh. But it had been almost intolerable to have a roomful of people discussing how the strength of his need was making him hallucinate. It was as if he had been coerced into stripping off his clothes and parading around naked, showing off some strange, slightly disgusting, slightly erotic growth on his body. No one had the right to such invasions of privacy. Not even Willy, really.

His mistake had been not to build up sufficient defenses, to speak to others of his art, assuming the others would have the sense to give him the dignity of distance. He had been friendly, including them, making his art seem a sort of communal thing, and it was not that way at all. This was not a topic for a committee and could not be passed around and democratized like the decisions for advertising copy for artwork. He was the one most at fault for talking about it in the first place. If he wanted them to leave him alone, he had to learn to deal with it—all of it—by himself. He could do that. He *would* do that.

Even deal with the ghost. God, what was she, after all, what did she do? Nothing so terrible, nothing destructive or harmful. She was an adolescent boy's fantasy, in a way. The beautiful woman who comes unbidden to do unspeakable things to his body in the middle of the night. If he couldn't deal with that by himself, what kind of man was he?

He had to change. Pull in. Withdraw. Isolate himself, delve into himself, if he was going to get any real work done. Willy could stand it; she knew what he was up to, and she could let him have that freedom, knowing that it was only another part of their lives together, only another time in their marriage. She knew how much he loved her. And she was strong, she had her own resources.

This time, John thought as he steered the car around the rotary toward the long road that paralleled the Cap Cod Canal, this time I'm really going to settle in and work. This time I'm serious. This time I'm not going to let anything stop me, not self-doubts or friendly temptations or ghostly interruptions.

THE FERRY APPROACHED OVER DARK WATER. FATHOMS DEEP LAY treasure, jewels and gold, sunken boats, lovers lost forever, their white bones gleaming, caught in the streaming seaweed, washed along with stones and rubies and brass buckles from belts and shoes, froth and plunder of the sea.

John leaned on the railing of the ferry, liking the cold slap of wet wind, the darkness. The lights of Nantucket were in the distance. Beneath him now lay mysteries, joys and terrors he could not imagine. And he thought how the land was all man knew of civilization and security; the sea was all he could bear to know of the wild, the amoral, the unguessed.

IT WAS JUST AFTER MIDNIGHT WHEN WILLY AND JOHN UNLOCKED their front door and entered their Orange Street house. It was silent inside, and cold, for they had left the heat turned down while they were gone.

They turned up the thermostat; then Willy, who was tired in spite of her nap in the car, headed for the bedroom.

"Coming?" she asked John, and when he shook his head and said he wasn't sleepy just yet, she only paused a moment, then swallowed whatever it was she had been going to say and went on into the bedroom alone.

John poured himself a brandy and soda and, keeping on his parka, because it would be coldest of all in the attic, where there was no heat, pulled on the light chain and went up the stairs into the cold, bright attic.

She was there, as he had thought she might be. She was in the darkest corner of the attic, without her cape now, dressed simply in a long dress of creamy, lacy cotton; and her hair was pulled back and up in thick, dark sloping loops secured with ivory-headed pins. Somehow it amused him that she had a shawl of gray wool wrapped loosely around her shoulders, as if she were guarding against the cold. As if a ghost could feel cold, or warmth.

"You've come back," she said, smiling, advancing just one step toward him. Her face was so beautiful, her expression so sweetly pleased by his presence.

"I've come back," he agreed. He had vowed to himself not to be afraid, not anymore, and it wasn't only fear that he felt now, really, though his heart knocked in his chest.

"It was cruel of you to go away," she said, again smiling that sweet smile, almost flirtatiously.

"It is cruel of you to come here," John responded, but he smiled, too, as he spoke to show this apparition he was friendly.

She drew back, surprised. "But this is my home!" she said.

"*Was* your home, perhaps," John said. "It's mine now— mine and my wife's."

98

The woman dropped her eyes. She was offended.

"I don't like your wife," she said petulantly, and then she let her shawl drop off one shoulder and trail to the ground. She began to wander around the attic, slowly, trailing her shawl along the ground as she walked. Every now and then she would glance sidelong at John, with a sweet, challenging smile, and as she turned this way and that, as she traced her seemingly aimless path, John realized that she was showing off for him. Showing off her winsome beauty. She was petite and very slender. Thin as a wraith, he thought, and smiled to himself at the expression. He thought he would easily be able to close his hands around her waist. Through the stuff of her dress he could see the push of her breasts, which were like a girl's, still small and high and peaked.

"Who are you?" he asked. "What's your name?"

"Such impertinence!" she said in reply, stopping still in her movement. She had turned toward him, full face, and she was indignant. A flush rose up her neck, a rosiness so vivid against her pale skin that John almost felt the heat of it. They were only a few feet apart. "This is *my* house. My dearest husband built it for *me*. For me to come into as his bride. And you ask who I am!"

She was so angry that John would not have been surprised if she had hit him; he felt her anger that strongly.

But she turned away and walked slowly back to the end of the attic. Her shawl still trailed gracefully over one arm, its feathery tips dancing against the wooden floor.

She stopped, looked over her shoulder at him, and now she was smiling again, a different sort of smile, a suggestive, provocative, openly sexual smile.

"Perhaps you should find out who I am," she said. "Perhaps you might like to make my acquaintance."

Then she was gone.

She had vanished, disappeared, before his eyes. Now John was not surprised. He had told himself he should expect such a thing, and now that it had happened, he really was not surprised. He was, though, admiring. And curious. But not unhappy. And strangely, not frightened anymore. He felt invigorated. But now he turned and went back down the stairs and stood next to the bed, where he stripped off his parka and clothes and let them fall into a pile where he stood. He sank heavily into bed next to Willy and fell asleep at once.

THE GREAT WHITE COLUMNED NEOCLASSIC LIBRARY, WITH THE NAME Atheneum announced in huge gold letters on the facade, looked forbiddingly grand compared to the modest village buildings surrounding it. Inside, it was surprisingly cozy. John was directed by a librarian to the section along the side of one wall that was devoted entirely to books on Nantucket. There were dozens. He selected a few of the oldest histories and carried them to a corner where the afternoon sun fell from high windows across the wooden table, making the yellow oak gleam.

There were entire books or sections of books devoted to the most famous families of the island, the Coffins and Starbucks and Macys and Husseys. There were ships' logs and chronicles and lists and charts and documents by the score, but it wasn't until the library was almost ready to close, two hours after he had started his search, that John found what he wanted. In a dog-eared, cottony-paged leather-bound book published in the 1920s, in the section entitled "Tragedies, Disasters and Bizarre Misfortunes," among tales of shipwrecks and mutinies, town fires and scandals, was an entry about "The Widowed Bride."

One of Nantucket's most romantic and saddest histories is that of Captain John Wright and Jesse Orsa Barnes.

Captain Wright met Miss Barnes in 1823 when he was twenty-four, a young Nantucket man who had just finished his first and extremely successful whaling cruise. Captain Wright had gone to Boston on legal matters and had visited at the home of relatives, where he met Miss Barnes, who was then seventeen and already known for her beauty. She is said to have been a slight, slender woman, graceful and delicate, with large dark eyes and long, thick, lustrous dark hair. (This in contrast to the descriptions of the island women, who, according to reports, tended to be large, husky, practical, and strong enough to perform the work of men—which, as their men were always gone, they had to do.)

Captain Wright was smitten at once and vowed to make young Miss Barnes his bride. He stayed on and on in Boston, delaying the next sailing of his ship, in order to meet Miss Barnes and persuade her to be his wife. Miss Barnes was reluctant to leave the society of Boston for the isolation of Nantucket, but Captain Wright persuaded her by saying that if she would be his wife, he would build her a fine, elegant home on Orange Street, which was where the "aristocracy" of Nantucket lived at that time. In addition, it must be stated that Captain Wright was himself a fine figure of a man, though not overly tall, still of noble bearing, and strikingly handsome, with blue eyes and dark hair and a graceful demeanor.

Finally, against the advice of her friends and guardian (for Miss Barnes was an orphan and an only child), she agreed to marry Captain Wright when he returned from his next whaling expedition. Miss Barnes's love for her fiancé must have been strong, for during the three years he was away, she was proposed to many times by men far wealthier than the captain, with far more to offer her in the way of culture and position and society. But for three years she waited for her affianced, attending only small gatherings and spending most of her time hand sewing her wedding trousseau.

In May 1826, Captain Wright returned home from his second and even more profitable whaling voyage. In the summer of that year the work was completed on the elegant neoclassic house he had had built on Orange Street, complete with servants' quarters, six fireplaces, and a widow's walk.

In September of that year, Captain Wright married Jesse Orsa Barnes in Christ Church in Cambridge, Massachusetts, and brought her home to Nantucket to live. Because Captain Wright was so wealthy, she had servants and did not have to perform menial tasks, as earlier Nantucket whaling wives had had to. It is reported that because of Jesse Orsa's beauty and refinement and education, she was shunned by the women of the island and considered to be haughty and even arrogant. And although the Quakerism of the island was waning at this time, still she was considered by the island to engage too often in frivolities and improprieties: She had her harmonium brought with her from Boston, and she often played and sang, with the windows open so that the music could drift out onto the streets and be heard by passersby. She had been seen, through those same open windows, dancing by herself to the tunes from her music box. She also drank liquor openly, engaged in smoking in her own house, and ordered books sent to her from the mainland that the librarian would never have allowed in the Atheneum. She rarely socialized with the island women and never attended any of the churches.

Captain Wright's ship, the *Parliament*, was due to leave Nantucket on another whaling cruise in November, but according to accounts, the departure was delayed time and time again due to Jesse Orsa's pleas to her new husband not to leave her so soon. It was said by those who visited the couple that never before had they seen a woman so obviously enamored of and devoted to her husband.

Unfortunately, Jesse Orsa was lucky to have detained her husband for as long as she did, for the *Parliament* left in the spring of 1827 and returned in the summer of 1830 with the tragic news that young Captain Wright was dead. He had not left his young bride with child when he set out, and so she had no child of his for solace. She had no friends on the island and no living relatives in all the world. She lived alone in her elegant, large house on Orange Street, the house her fiancé had promised her if she would be his bride, until she died at the age of eighty-one, a lonely and bitter woman.

Here the account ended at the top of the page so that on the left page and the right two portraits could be shown, in black and white: oils of Jesse Orsa Wright and Captain John Wright. John Constable stared at the pictures, transfixed. There was no denying the remarkable resemblance between himself and the young captain. And there was no denying that the picture of "The Widowed Bride" was a picture of the ghost, the beautiful young apparition he had spoken with only the night before.

He was so stunned that he did not think to turn the page, to read on, to see if the account continued.

AT DINNER THAT NIGHT HE COULD SCARCELY HEAR WHAT WILLY SAID, scarcely force himself to respond intelligently. He was obsessed with what he had learned and thought over and over again: I am not mad. I am not hallucinating. She does exist. She does exist.

HE WENT TO THE ATTIC THAT NIGHT.

The woman was standing by the window, gazing out at the dark harbor. Her hair was loosened and hung in shining waves down to her waist. John thought she was wearing the same cotton dress she had worn the night before, but when she turned, he saw that instead she wore a cotton nightgown. It fell from many tiny pleats at the shoulders, over the small pronounced bosom, to the floor. Lacework intricately edged the shoulders and collar and cuffs, and while it was a discreet gown, it was also alluring, because its sheerness made obvious the fact that the woman wore no undergarments.

John cleared his throat. He was excited, frightened, aroused.

"You are here," he said, smiling.

The woman returned his smile. "Yes," she said. "I am always here—waiting."

"I know who you are now," John said. "Jesse Orsa Wright." When she did not reply, he continued. "The widowed bride of Captain John Wright, who died at sea during his third command."

He was surprised to see how she lowered her lids at that, and twisted her mouth, so that she looked sardonic, even bitter.

"You are such a gentleman," she said.

John paused, uncertain what she meant by the remark. Then he said, "I should introduce myself. I'm John Constable."

Again that bitter smile.

"I like your name," she said.

"I like yours," he replied. Then, more boldly, "There are so many questions I would like to ask you."

"There are so very few of them I'll be able to answer," she said, still smiling. "But we can talk. I would like to talk with you. I would like that very much. Yet—" She tilted her head, obviously deliberating. "Yet," she continued, "how can we talk? There is not even a place for us to sit. Do you mean for us to remain standing for the rest of our time together?"

"I—I didn't mean, hadn't thought—" John stumbled, surprised and confused at this turn of conversation.

"A chair would be nice," she said. "Two chairs. And perhaps a rug. A table? A crystal decanter of brandy?"

"Oh, well—come downstairs!" John said. "All that is downstairs. It's much more comfortably set up down there."

The woman shook her head impatiently. "I don't *want* to be down there," she said, and again a petulant note entered into the sweet lilt of her voice. "You've already changed all that so much. It's hers. As much as yours, as much as mine. But here—here—" She came closer to him. She came quickly closer, so close he could have reached out and touched her, so close he could smell the agreeable, strangely spicy, unfamiliar smell of his dreams of her. "This could be our place," she said. "Ours."

"Yes, of course," he agreed readily. "It will be. I'll do anything. What would you like?"

"Chairs," she said, smiling, turning slowly to look around the attic. John stood still, openly staring at her without blinking, as if the strength of his stare could make her disappear if she were not real. But she was real. He could not see through her. He could smell her. He could almost feel her warmth. He could tell how the lace of her nightgown was different in texture from the creamy-smooth surface of her skin. He could see the pulse beating in the side of her throat. He could see the blue veins beneath her white skin.

"And a rug," she continued, turning back. Her smile indicated that she knew he had been studying her. "A table, a crystal decanter of brandy. I like chocolates, too. And . . . of course . . . John . . ." she said, and paused and let the smile drop from her face. They were caught looking at each other with all seriousness then, and John could feel that seriousness deepening inside him like the hue of the evening sky changing from light blue to indigo, so that the darkness stained his blood.

"We'll need a bed," she said.

She continued to gaze at him steadily, seriously, for a few more moments after she had spoken; she kept him spellbound. Then, when he raised his hand to touch her, she vanished, but not before giving him a brief, satisfied smile.

NOW HE DID NOT LET HIMSELF THINK OR QUESTION. THERE WERE times in life when such blind obedience to a superior force was necessary: as an infant, in the armed services, in school. There was no question of choice. There was no question of values. He had been caught up in something miraculous. If he thought to himself, What kind of man spends his wife's money to furnish a room for an affair with another woman? he pushed the thought aside. He was now beyond turning back.

WILLY'S CHEEKS BURNED WITH COLD.

"This is crazy!" she shouted, but John was already too far ahead of her to hear. That was how she felt he *always* was recently, going on along all on his own, too fast for her to follow, out of the reach of her voice.

She had agreed to come biking with him on this brisk January day simply because she thought the exercise would ease the tension that ran through him these days, making him edgy and impolite. So she had bundled up in long underwear and jeans and sweaters and her parka and gloves, but still it was fiercely cold. And here, by the water, it was painfully so.

She brought her bike to a stop at the end of the street and looked out across the long stretch of sand to the water lapping gently at the Jetties beach. Long grass the color of sand waved stiffly when the wind hit it, and a loose shingle or shutter on the boarded-up concession stand softly thumped like an insistent, irregular heart. The sky and sea were a heathery hue, everything was still, and far out shone a glaze of approaching white, promising that the snow that was now layering the Cape would soon be here.

Willy sighed. It was so lonely here now, it was melancholy. *She* was lonely, melancholy. She and John had had a fight this morning, not over his buying all the expensive furniture for the attic but over his impatience for its delivery.

"You've gone this long without it—you didn't even want it until we came back from Boston—why get so upset about it, John?" she had asked, trying to be reasonable. But her reasoning, her attempts to calm him, had only infuriated him all the more.

The rug had arrived. It was an antique, different from anything Willy had ever thought John would like. It was a French design of flowers and fleur-de-lis on creamy wool. Two small armchairs in shiny striped brocades had also been carried up to the attic. And a mahogany side table with scalloped edges and ivory inlay.

What John was waiting for with such impatience was a bed.

He had been waiting for a week now, and it still hadn't arrived from the mainland.

When Willy questioned John, the first time she so much as lightly mentioned all his purchases, he had blown up at her.

"You've repainted your sewing room!" he said, defensive. "Look at it! You've got an armchair, an Oriental rug, and how much did those drapes cost! So you can sit and *sew*! I'm trying to be an artist—do I have to do it in a stark attic? Do I have to try to create beauty in an atmosphere of ugliness?"

"John—" Willy had interrupted. "Hey, John. Wait a minute. What are you so angry about? I was only asking—"

He had bought three electric heaters from Marine Home Center, tan radiator-looking appliances filled with mineral oil, and carried them up the stairs himself. He told Willy they made a huge difference; at last he was comfortable there. He found several old large tables at Island Attics and now had his paints and brushes and pads and pens set out in easy reach.

The last time Willy had been up to the attic, she could see that it was getting shaped up nicely. At one end, by the window looking out at the harbor, were his easels and tables and paints—the working end. At the other end of the attic, the shadowy end, were the rug, the chairs and table, and a crystal decanter filled with cognac set on a silver tray. The relaxing end, Willy supposed.

There were two small, etched, silver-rimmed wineglasses on the silver tray.

"*Two* glasses?" Willy had asked, smiling. "Are you planning to invite me up sometime to view your etchings?"

"No!" John had answered abruptly. Then, seeing the expression on Willy's face, he had apologized. "God, I'm sorry. I'm a maniac. I mean, yes, of course, exactly. Willy, God, I'm sorry."

The apology had come yesterday. Today there had been no apology for his quick temper, his general surliness. The closest he had come to apologizing was to invite her along on this bike ride. "Perhaps I just need the exercise," he had said.

And Willy had bundled up and come along. But he was not with her, not really, not now while he was physically so far off in the distance and not even when he had been pedaling at her side—then his thoughts had clearly been on other things.

What those other things might be he could not seem to tell her. John was more closed off to her now than he had ever been at any point in their life together. She could not even guess what was going on.

Or, rather, she could guess, but it was all so ludicrous, so absurd. So *impossible.*

Willy reminded herself of the promise she had made to herself on the trip back from Boston, how she had vowed to leave John alone, to let him have his muse or ghost or whatever it was in peace and privacy so that he could get on with his work.

Yet in her mind she was constantly troubled. She had to force herself every minute to remain calm, not to bother him about it all, not to question.

Not to ask: John, are you getting a bed up in the attic so you can sleep with that ghost of yours?

Then, in the act of stating the question, even in the silence of her mind, the foolishness of the question amused her, and she would laugh out loud, her common sense returning. It made Willy smile to herself even here on the beach with the wind buffeting her. All this was ridiculous, her fears were ridiculous, people didn't have affairs with *ghosts*. How could she be so silly?

A gust of wind hit her again, and she turned her bike and began to pedal back home. John had already disappeared down the long stretch of road. He had gone off without her. Well, that was all right, that was all right, they were two separate people. And if he was being impatient lately, and rude and preoccupied, well, that would pass. She had never lived with him when he was really working.

Willy was working, too; a church in Boston had commissioned a banner of the seasons for their chancel. It was to be the largest piece she'd ever done and would involve felt and other pieces of material as well as threads. As she biked along, now quite uncomfortable as the cold metal of the handlebars stung through the protection of her gloves and the icy air she breathed seared her lungs, she comforted herself with thoughts of the banner. Trees, fruits, flowers, birds, beasts, a riot of colors would be needed, and she would weave the seasons in a circle so that one would intertwine with the next.

It would be like marriage, Willy thought. There are seasons in marriage, too. Now we are in winter for a while, but spring will come.

CHAPTER SIX

I T HAD BEEN TEN DAYS SINCE HE HAD SEEN HER.

Tonight, he was sure, she would come. It was true that for the past ten nights he had felt just this way, sure that she would appear. But tonight—tonight was different, because today the bed had been delivered.

He did not know what was happening. His life had become a dream, a series of brute movements through a muted world, as if he were a great, dumb sea beast swimming in thick, dark depths. He slept. He ate. He drank, more than he should. Twice during the past ten days, after he had waited and waited in the attic and still she had not come, he had gone to bed and fucked Willy; it could not have been called making love.

And he had painted, was painting. At least there was that. It was seeming to come without his conscious thought, the work he was doing now; he did not plan it but worked spontaneously, as if something stronger were guiding his hand. He was painting on a large canvas, eight feet square, a night scene in deep blues and black with gradations of gray and touches of silver for illumination. The harbor at night, the towering and complicated masts of fishing boats looming into the sky, the eerie line of lights of the long, low ferry as it rounded Brant Point, only its windows and its approach lights shining through the dark, the cold January moon darkened by smoky clouds that possessed the air. He was not finished; it was a difficult painting. There were lines he needed to get right, and subtleties of shading. But when he finished working each day, he felt exhausted and pleased.

It was nine-thirty. Willy was out. She had been going to church each Sunday and had met some women who were part of a book club; tonight she was attending one of their meetings. So he was alone in the house.

Everything was here at last: the rug, the chairs, the table, the glasses, the crystal decanter with the finest brandy—the bed. He had ordered expensive sheets of lace-trimmed cream-colored cotton and a matching thick cream colored quilt. How Willy had raised her eyebrows when she saw him unpacking that from the box!

"Not quite your style, I would have thought," she had said, her voice light, but he had seen, when she turned away, how a shade of sorrow fell across her face, so that in one instant she looked older. Guilt surged through John.

"Well," he said, "it was the first thing I came across in the catalog," which was, after all, true.

"Do you want some help making up the bed?" Willy had asked. Her back had been to him. He could not see her face. But her voice had sounded normal, easy.

"No, thanks," he answered, trying to keep his voice equally easy. He knew he should say more, should tell her to come up and see what the attic looked like now that everything was in place. But he could not bring himself to do it. Yet he needed to say something to her.

"Willy, I love you," he said, meaning it.

They were in the front hall, the box of bedding from Bloomingdale's between them. John was on his way up to the attic, Willy at the other end of the hall, going into the living room. She turned and looked at John and gave him a smile of delight.

"Oh, Johnny, I love you, too," she said.

And he had gone up the stairs into the attic to make the bed, thinking how glad he was that Willy was so even-tempered and sweet and good and thinking at the same time what a traitor he was.

Dinner that evening passed quickly. Willy discussed the book she had finished reading in time for the book club meeting, and John managed to focus his thoughts enough to make adequate responses. Then she had gone off cheerfully into the night, and now at last here he was, alone in the house, sitting in one of the new, expensive brocade chairs, waiting.

Waiting for a ghost.

The waiting was in itself an act as consuming as any he'd ever committed. Vaguely he was aware of the oddness of it all, of the process he was involved in, how he could not seem to think about the significance of this, how he no longer asked himself questions about what all this meant: a ghost, afterlife, a God, heaven, hell. If he tried to force himself to such thoughts, he found he fell asleep or grew restless and could not concentrate. His mind had become both dulled and jazzed up at once, for while he could not think about spiritual matters, he found himself obsessed with the physical. The carnal. He was like an adolescent again, daydreaming endlessly about Jesse Orsa Wright, remembering the slenderness of her waist, the firm, high breasts that swelled beneath the fine cotton of her garments. Only when he was painting was he free of thoughts of her, although the energy to paint came, he knew, from the same source as those thoughts.

But every other hour of his life now, waking or sleeping, was filled with a constant replaying of all he had come to know so far of this woman through his senses of sight and smell and sound. He was not yet sure if he had also felt and tasted her; he was not sure if his dreams of her teasing visits before Christmas had been merely dreams or real visits. He was no longer sure of anything. Reality had blurred for him and lost all its boundaries.

So he sat and waited and replayed in his mind the last time he had seen her, how she had come so close to him that he could feel her warmth.

Now he thought he heard music. The tinkling of a piano . . . No, it was a more delicate sound, a sweeter, higher, trilling sound. The sound of a music box. He half rose from his chair, straining to hear where the music came from. It seemed to be coming from downstairs, from his own living room, where there was no music box. Then the door to the attic opened, and he could hear the music clearly now.

The door to the attic shut, and the music diminished, disappeared, and Jesse Orsa came up the stairs, lifting the full skirt of her gown, humming the same tune he had just heard. She was dressed as if for a party, in a gown of pink satin and white lace that fell off her shoulders, revealing smooth young flesh, the gentle line of her collarbone, the soft hollow of her throat. The alluring swell of lace-covered breasts. Her hair was done up with great intricacy and adorned with bits of ribbon, lace, and combs of ivory, and she had pearls hanging from her ears and a choker of pearls around her neck. She came up the stairs, laughing.

John rose, aware all of a sudden of his shabbiness; he was wearing old faded jeans, a button-down shirt frayed at the collar and cuffs, a shapeless old crewneck sweater. He had not thought anything of what he would wear when he saw her again, but now he was embarrassed.

"You look so beautiful," he exclaimed.

Jesse Orsa smiled, very gay, her whole manner that of any beautiful woman who has just come from a party.

"Well, all this is lovely!" she said, sweeping past him to

circle the little civilized area he had made of rug and furniture. "Yes, *very* nice. Thank you, John. You deserve a kiss for that!"

And before he could catch his breath, she came close to him and kissed his mouth, with exquisite skill, not pecking, not lingering, touching long enough that he could feel her lips, her breath. Her sweet breath. His own breath caught in his throat. She whirled away, energetic, festive, triumphant, like a beautiful woman just coming from a party where she was much admired.

"Will you—will you sit down? Have some cognac?" John asked, uncertain about what to do next.

"Oh, I wish I could," she said. "But I'm in a hurry tonight. Tomorrow, perhaps?" She was now at the other end of the room, by the bed, in the shadows.

"In a hurry?" John asked, speaking the first thought that came into his mind. "But good God, where can you possibly have to go?"

In a flash her mood changed from gaiety to anger; he could feel it across the distance of the attic. She tossed her head and glared at him.

"OH!" she exclaimed, and stamped her foot once. "You are so insolent!"

And she vanished.

"Well, *damn*!" John said aloud. He walked toward the place where she had stood. "Hey—Jesse Orsa—come back here! Please. Please come back. Look, I've gone to all this trouble. Don't you like—Oh, shit," John finished in exasperation. He could not believe that the encounter he had anticipated for ten days now had come and gone with such unsatisfactory quickness. He paced around the attic, hitting his fists together, trying to expel the energy of frustration that shot through him now.

"This is stupid, stupid," he muttered to himself. "This is pointless, ridiculous, this is a joke!"

THAT NIGHT, WHEN WILLY CAME HOME, SHE FOUND JOHN IN FRONT OF the TV. This was a nice surprise for her, because recently he seemed to spend all his time in the attic in the evenings and sometimes didn't come down until so late that she had fallen asleep in bed with the light on, waiting for him.

"We had a wonderful meeting," she said happily, coming to sit next to her husband on the sofa. He smelled strongly of scotch, and she hoped he hadn't been drinking, hoped he wasn't starting "to drink."

But he turned to her and looked at her with such somberness that she was sure he was sober.

"Oh, Willy," he said with an odd sadness in his voice. He pulled her to him and began to kiss her. He began to make love to her, there on the living room sofa with the television still blaring away, distracting her, and she tried to pull away, to tell John this, that she wanted to go up to the bedroom, but he didn't seem interested in pleasing her tonight, but came to her, into her, in a childish, selfish way, as if comforting himself with her body. He removed her sweater, rubbed her breasts, entered her without removing his jeans, wallowed in her, really, while she could only lie there, almost amused, certainly touched and overwhelmed by his silent, powerful need. She lay there cuddling him against her, soothing him, letting him take his time, while the TV sang and rambled and the windowpanes shook relentlessly with the night's wind.

JOHN PAINTED EVERY DAY. HE WAITED IN THE ATTIC EVERY NIGHT.

The woman appeared the third night. She was wearing a proper, plain daytime dress of gray and had her hair up, arranged neatly. John, seated in one of the brocade armchairs, saw her suddenly standing at the top of the stairs, her hands clasped before her breasts. She wore a cameo brooch at her neck. For all the severity of her appearance, she was still very beautiful.

"Are you still angry with me?" he asked, standing.

"Yes," she said quietly. "For *many* reasons."

"But *I* should be angry with *you!*" John said. He was speaking softly, for Willy was in the house, downstairs in their bedroom, reading. He was glad that their bedroom was not directly under this part of the attic. "You come and go without warning, you make me wait for you without any clue or hope or arrangement . . . I've gone to all this trouble to please you, and then you come only once in two weeks—I don't understand. At least let me know what it is you want."

"What it is I want?" she repeated his words slowly. She came across the wooden floor and stepped onto the soft, deep carpet. John thought she would touch him now, for she came so close to him, her face serious, her eyes holding his. Then a private sort of smile crossed her face, and she turned from him and went to sink gracefully into a chair.

"For now, I think, what I would like is some of your cognac," she said.

He poured it. He handed her the delicate, etched crystal glass. He watched her bring it to her lips and sip.

He thought: When the glass is sitting empty on the table, that will be my proof that she has come and drunk and gone, that she does exist. That she can engage in physical activities.

Her eyes were amused. Then she said, merely, "John." She sipped her cognac, then gently put the glass back down on the table. She sat looking at him.

And he rose from where he had been seated in his chair across the little mahogany-and-ivory table from her and crossed the small space between them and took her shoulders in his hands and pulled her up from her chair and pulled her body against his and kissed her mouth while holding her head to his with his hand. She came willingly against him and returned his kiss.

He kissed her fervently, running his hands over her shoulders, neck, arms, back, pushing her buttocks so that her pelvis rubbed through her skirts against him. He moved his hands against her small waist, up her rib cage, and finally he fondled her breasts through the thick barrier of material.

He had thought she would resist him, reproach him, for she was angered so easily and she was so old-fashioned, he did not know her rules. But she did not stop him. While she did not stroke him back, she did not push him away, and instead she let him touch her and kiss her while making little moaning noises in her throat.

"You are real, you are real," he whispered into her hair, against her neck. Bending down, he nuzzled his face into her breasts. "You are real. My God, I can feel you. You are real."

She pulled back a little so that she could look into his face. She was smiling, her eyes sparkling, her face rosy with sexual heat. "Yes," she said. "Yes. Go on. See how real I am."

She had to help him, for her clothes were strange to him and he was clumsy with the small buttons of bone and the strange lacings and ribbons that held together the garments that covered her. She was equally curious, then gleeful about his clothes. But finally they were naked together on the thick, warm rug. They stood looking at each other with the same sense of wonder and awe that all new lovers feel. John's heart was pounding away furiously inside his body, and he knew that he was trembling—with lust, with fear. But he could feel Jesse Orsa trembling, too.

"I want to make love to you," he whispered, pulling her against him. "I want to take you to bed."

In reply, she raised her arms around his neck and lay her head on his shoulder. When he picked her up in his arms, she felt as light as a child. When he lay her down on the bed, she simply reclined there and let him look at her. Her eyes were shining, her lips were moist, her cheeks and neck and chest were flushed. She was very small but so very beautiful. She was flawless, without a mark on her anywhere. Her flesh was alabaster, smooth, taut, her nipples dark brown and hard as marbles. She smelled sweet, like grass and spice and flowers. She was warm and moist and giving. He sank down onto the bed and covered her body with his.

Her hair came loose from its fastenings while they made love, and near her face it curled where moistened by sweat or her tears or his kisses. It fell in coils and clumps against her shoulders and breasts when she rose above him, and when he was above her, it spread across the pillow in deep swirls of fragrant black. He moved against her on and on while she ran her hands over his face and body, whispering his name and begging him not to stop. He did not want to stop, not ever, not while he felt such pleasure, not while he was giving such pleasure to her. At last she called his name, then turned her head and sank her teeth into his shoulder while arching helplessly, ecstatically, against him. He moaned and climaxed and subsided against her.

He was afraid for one moment that she might vanish now, but she stayed, stayed with him, petting him, stroking him, kissing him, praising him, rubbing her face and hair and hands against him, thanking him, caressing him, laughing now, triumphant, joyful, released, fulfilled.

"Oh, John, my John, my love, I love you, I love you," she said over and over again. "You make me so happy, you make me so happy, I love you," she said.

Finally, exhausted, they lay together holding each other, and in spite of himself, not meaning to, meaning *not* to, John fell asleep.

When he awoke, he was alone. He was alone, and naked in the bed, which was rumpled and mussed. He raised up on one elbow and looked around. She was nowhere around, nor were her clothes. The attic was quiet, the windows dark with night. He looked at his watch. It was only one o'clock. It seemed to him that it could be any time at all, any night in any century, he felt so disoriented and drained. Slowly he sat up and gathered together his thoughts. He felt absolutely depleted, as if he had just run a marathon.

On the ivory-and-mahogany table were the two glasses, both half full. But no, how foolish, that could not be proof that she had come—*he* could have drunk the sherry. What, then? He rose and shook out the sheets, hoping to find something, a pin, a comb, a ribbon, even a strand of hair. Naked, he stalked around the attic, peering at the chair she had sat in, the rug where she had stood, and back to the bed where they had lain together. There was nothing, no sign at all that she had been there.

It was only when he slowly, achingly, began to dress, forcing himself to move against his exhaustion, that he saw the small bruise she had made on his shoulder with her teeth. He could not have done that himself; he could not have reached that place with his own mouth.

AND TONIGHT, DAMN IT, WILLY WAS AWAKE WHEN HE CAME INTO THE bedroom. The lamp on her bedside table was on, and she was reading, propped against pillows. When he entered the room, she raised her head and stretched and yawned.

"John?" she questioned. "What time is it?"

"Late," he replied. "Go back to sleep." They both were speaking softly. He had dressed in the attic a few minutes before; now he stood by his closet and took off the clothes he had just put on. He managed to slip into his pajama top with his back still turned to Willy, so that he was buttoning it when he turned to her. So she could not see the mark Jesse Orsa's teeth had left.

"John," Willy said as her husband slipped in next to her and sank down, groaning into the comfort of the warm bed. "Is something wrong?"

"Wrong? No, of course not," John said, keeping his voice normal. "I just fell asleep up there, honey." He forced himself to turn toward her, to look at her. For the first time in his life he did not want to touch his wife, but he made himself reach out and stroke her arm. Her hair was down, falling loose over her plump shoulder, and she was wearing one of her sexy, sheer lacy nightgowns, the sort of thing she seldom wore in the winter when it was so cold. "I know it's odd," he went on, speaking to her unspoken questions. "I didn't know I'd end up working at all hours like this. It's so hard to explain . . . how the ideas and the energy come. I—I work awhile, and then I get so tired, and I either sit down and rest, or tonight I just lay down and fell asleep on the bed awhile. Then woke up and knew exactly what I want to do to finish the painting. I'm almost finished. And it's good and it's different."

"I'm so glad," Willy said. She reached out to caress John's face. She smoothed his hair. "I'm so glad your work is going well for you."

She moved closer to him in the bed, nudging her bosom against his chest. Her legs softly slid against his. She brought her face to his, meaning to touch her lips to his, but he drew his face back, turned his head away.

"No, Willy, please," he said, more sharply than he meant to. "I'm tired," he said.

Willy pulled back, all the way back, removing every bit of her body from his. The expression on her face changed completely. She had been soft, loving, lovely; now she looked puzzled and angry and sad.

"Johnny—" she began.

"Please, Willy," John said, forestalling her. Again he forced himself to reach out and touch her arm. "Please understand. I'm exhausted. Wait till you see what I've done, I think you'll understand then. Or maybe I'm coming down with a cold. Don't be angry. I just have to sleep. Okay?"

"Okay," Willy said, but her eyes were worried. She pulled away from John and turned out the bedside lamp.

John immediately fell into a churning dark sleep. Willy lay beside him, staring into the dark night, wondering.

~~~~~~~~

THE NEXT DAY, JOHN FINISHED THE NIGHT HARBOR SCENE AND started a new canvas. Again it was a night scene, an ocean scene, this time from the perspective of a boat approaching land, approaching the town of Nantucket where the land rose in a gentle sweep, with the gold dome of South Church crowning the arch. In this painting all the houses were gray shingle, and it was late, dark, and foggy, so that the houses on land seemed to float and fade and waver with the same sliding insubstantiality of their reflection in the dark water. Everything was gray or black except for the gold dome of the church, which was washed in a cold sweep of moonlight that deadened the gold sheen to a gloomy near white.

Willy came up to see what John had done. "Oh, John, this is quite powerful," she said about the finished canvas. "And this—it will have more color in it, won't it? Doesn't it seem a bit . . . *dark* as it is now?"

"It's meant to be dark," John answered. "I like it dark."

It was after dinner. They had eaten in a friendly silence, drinking lots of wine, and John, relaxed, yet anticipating the night when Jesse Orsa would come again, had invited Willy up to the attic to see what he had accomplished. So she would know he was working, he thought in the back of his mind. So she would understand why he was so preoccupied, so tired. So she would leave him alone.

Now Willy came up behind John and wrapped her arms around his waist, pressing her face against his back. "Mmm," she said, nuzzling him. "You're so warm. Come down to bed now, sweetheart."

"I can't, Willy," John said, tensing at her touch. "I want to work some more."

"But you've worked all day," she complained. "You've done so much. Come relax for just a little while. . . ." She moved her hands down his torso until they touched his crotch. "Come down to the bedroom just for a while. Then you can come back up to work."

His body did not respond to her touch. He stood very still, feeling cold and distant from his wife.

"Willy," he said, "I want to work. If I come down now, I won't be able to; the impetus will be gone."

Willy let her arms fall away from her husband's body and stepped back. For one moment she was tempted just to walk off down the stairs in complete silence, letting that silence speak for her anger and pique. But she loved him so, and he had been working so hard. These pictures he was doing now—she might not care for them, she might find them dreary, even unpleasant, but she was no judge of art, and she had no idea how much this work was taking out of him. She had promised herself that she would help John in his attempt to work; that meant being good-humored even now, at times like this, when he was ignoring her.

"All right, Johnny," she said, keeping her voice pleasant. "I'll go on down and let you get back to work."

As she turned, she saw the other end of the attic, which was in shadows now that the lights were off; she saw the two glasses on the table. She saw the rumpled bed. A cold spasm constricted her heart, a cramp of fear. But what was it she was afraid of? She warned herself against foolishness and went on down the stairs.

John painted for a while, though he was not wholly concentrating; he kept looking at his watch. It was after nine, then after ten—she had come last night around ten. Then it was after eleven. He stopped painting, for he could think of nothing else but whether she would come or make him wait another night. He cleaned his brushes, straightened his work area.

Finally, when he heard the town clock striking midnight, twelve golden strokes, he looked over to see Jesse Orsa seated in one of the chairs. She was wearing a dressing gown of dark purple velvet with black fur cuffs and collar. And nothing underneath. Her hair was tied back with a purple ribbon.

He crossed the room and knelt before her, taking her hands in his.

"I was afraid you weren't coming," he said.

"I meant not to come," she replied. "I meant to stay away. I don't want you to get tired of me, bored with me," she said.

"Oh, *Christ*," John said, "Christ, Jesse Orsa. You know I could never get tired of you. My God."

He untied her robe and parted it away from her naked body, and as she sat there, he kissed her all over, burying his head in her sweetness, breathing in the scent of her as if it were the breath of life.

~~~~~~~~

IN THE NEXT TWO WEEKS, SHE CAME TO THE ATTIC SEVEN TIMES. THE nights she didn't come, he fell asleep on the bed to awaken at three or four, cold and stiff and disoriented. He would go down to the second-floor bedroom to finish sleeping with Willy. The nights she did come, they made love for hours, so that he stumbled, nearly sick with love, into bed far after midnight.

Willy did not question him. He was grateful for that; gratitude was the best emotion he could muster toward Willy these days. He was wild with lovesickness for Jesse Orsa; he was overcome with lust.

Some nights they talked a little before they fell asleep or

while they were making love. It was John who initiated the talking, every time.

"Tell me who you are," he would beg, holding this small woman from him for a moment, searching her face.

"You know who I am," she would say, smiling, her face all innocence and love.

"But how can you be here? I don't understand."

"You don't need to understand. Why must you *under-stand*? Isn't it enough that I am here?" she would ask, and pull him to her so that he would cover her with kisses in answer.

Another time, when he was in her, thrusting into her, he looked down at her and said angrily, "You are a ghost, aren't you? Tell me. You are a *ghost.*" He was holding her arms down with his hands.

"I am a ghost," she said, not smiling. Her eyes, her dark eyes, were black with depth. "But I am real. I am real."

And another time, when she was on top of him, moving in slow glides, her bare arms raised, holding her thick, long hair up away from her breasts so that he could see all of her—even then he knew she was proud of herself, narcissistic. That time, when she was making him crazy with sexual pleasure, he clasped her thighs and said, "I'll do anything for you. I don't know who you are or what you want, but I'll do anything for you. I'll give you anything. Anything."

She bent to kiss him, and they talked no more that night.

The night before, when they were together, after they had finished making love, he lay looking down at her, where she was gracefully collapsed onto the bed, her body rosy from sexual heat. Her eyes were closed. He studied her.

"How is it you can be here?" he asked, running his hand over her smooth, flat stomach. "How is it you can be here, so truly *here,* and then vanish so completely?"

"It's a miracle," she told him, opening her eyes, smiling. "Truly it is, John. A miracle. Can't you accept that and let the wondrousness of it convince you that it is right?"

"But I want to understand," he protested. "Jesse Orsa Wright, you lived a century ago, and yet you are here now, a ghost, and yet a living, breathing woman. How can this be? I want to know."

"John," she said, raising up and touching his face with one slender hand, "don't be impatient. Please. I promise you that soon . . . *soon* . . . you will know all that I know."

HE HAD A NEW ROUTINE NOW. HE SLEPT LATE INTO THE MORNING, deep, sinking, possessing sleeps of exhaustion. When he awoke around eleven, he showered, dressed, and walked to the Hub to buy the morning papers. He returned home and read the papers and the mail while he drank coffee. Then he went to the attic. He worked at odd jobs there, cleaning his brushes, sketching ideas; the real work he saved for the night. He spent most of the afternoon asleep on the bed in the attic; it seemed he could not get enough sleep.

It was now February. Carpenters were pounding away in the kitchen and the library, taking up a great deal of Willy's time and attention and direction. John was grateful for this and for the fact that she seemed to think their noise and general chaos were driving him up to the third floor.

He would awaken around five, when the windows were black with night. Then he would paint, working like a man driven. He finished the nighttime harbor scene and painted a church and churchyard at night. Moonlight fell on the winding brick path leading to the chapel door. It was in depths of gray, all of it. He knew it was eerie but did not mind.

By seven, he would force himself away from his canvas and downstairs to eat dinner with Willy. Television helped him; helped him keep up a semblance of normalcy with her. That and the newspapers—he could discuss the news of the real world. He had little appetite these days, and Willy was worried, he could tell, worried and slightly offended. But food did not interest him at all. Still, he forced himself to eat, to talk, to smile, to joke with his wife, who had somehow become a bother in his real life.

After dinner and some amount of time spent with Willy so that she would not be suspicious, John would go back to the attic to paint. And to wait. And two more weeks went by in this way, as if in a dream or a fever.

One night he said to Jesse Orsa as they lay together in the mussed bed, "Do you like my paintings?"

"Oh!" she said, offended, and drew back. She had been kissing his chest. "How can you talk about paintings *now*! *They* don't interest me. *You* are all that interests me."

But I am an artist, he wanted to say. Those paintings are part of me. Yet he did not speak. He had offended her, and he had to take her in an ardent embrace so that she would not leave him. Still, she had hurt his feelings. He had somehow assumed that because she loved him so, she would care about his paintings.

Later, after they made love, he tried to express all this to her. But she laughed at him, then grew serious, her eyes dark. "John," she said, "what men do on this earth doesn't matter— not painting or possessing or commanding. Only this matters— what we have between the two of us."

"But it has to matter," he protested. "A little. Love is important, but it isn't everything, is it?"

And so quickly he had made her angry. She drew herself up, began to slip into the heavy purple velvet robe. "I'll let you decide," she said. "I'll leave you to your paintings, and you see what it is that matters to you."

She was gone.

She did not come back for a week. He thought he would go wild with desire, impatience, and the fear that she had left him for good.

When she returned, their lovemaking was a feast, a gluttony.

"You must never leave me again for so long," he begged, pressing her to him, speaking into her hair. "You must never leave me that way again. I need you, Jesse Orsa. I need you. I must have you."

She wrapped herself around him. "I need you, too, John," she whispered, her breath in his ear. "I must have you, too."

CHAPTER SEVEN

WILLY HAD GRILLED PORTERHOUSE STEAKS WITH MUSHROOMS and wine and served them with wild rice and a green salad in a pungent oil-and-vinegar sauce. John had eaten almost nothing, and Willy ate hers and then finally all of his, too, as if defending her food.

It was almost eight-thirty. The carpenters had worked late in the house, delaying their dinner.

John pushed his chair back from the table.

"Well, I guess I'll go up to the attic and work for a while," he said.

"No," Willy said.

John looked at his wife, surprised. "Willy, I have work to do," he said.

"Not tonight," she said. "Please, John. I mean it. Not tonight."

"Willy—" John began.

"Stop it!" Willy interrupted him. "Don't even begin with your excuses."

"Excuses," John said, angry now. "Hell, Willy, what do you mean, excuses? I'm working. You've seen what I'm doing. What the hell are you talking about?"

"I'm talking about the fact that we haven't made love in over a month!" Willy said. Suddenly there were tears in her eyes. "Never mind that you never speak to me about what you're thinking these days or about anything important to you. Anything *private.* Oh, you talk to me—you made a point to talk to me, little *recitatives* about politics and the local news! I can see you, Johnny, thinking: Well, now I've talked with Willy for fifteen minutes, that ought to hold her for another night, now I can escape to the attic!"

"Oh, Willy," John said, and slumped in his chair, depressed.

"John," Willy went on, her voice softer, her face earnest. "I'm so worried about you. Not just because you're ignoring me, although I hate that. I hate being so cut off from you, it's terrible—"

"Willy," John began.

"No, hear me out. I *hate* it that you've cut me off so completely, and I think it's wrong. I think you would agree if you could look at it rationally. How close we've been for years, lovers, best friends, everything to each other . . . and now, suddenly . . . you've put such a distance between us. Why? Can you tell me why? *Will* you tell me why? When you look at me, John, you look as if you're seeing a stranger. And one you don't particularly want to know."

Willy's voice was so gentle, so sad. John looked at his wife. There she sat, his big, substantial, sensible wife, with her blond hair in its practical lump of a braid. Her broad forehead was shiny, her eyes red with withheld tears, her nose reddened, too. Under her thick, coarse, heavy sweater lay her great whomping breasts. He looked at his wife and could not imagine how he had ever loved her.

But he did not want to be unkind. And some odd sense

within him warned him not to anger her now; he did not want an upheaval in his life just now.

"Willy—" he began weakly, not knowing what to say. "Please be patient with me. I know this is hard for you, a change for you—" Please leave me alone, he wanted to plead. But how could he ask that without offending her?

Tears shimmered in Willy's eyes. "John, let me finish," she said. "It's not just me, how you are with me. *I love you.* I'm your wife and I love you, and I'll never stop loving you. I can take it, this distance you've put between us, I can stand all this—for a while. But Johnny, I'm worried about *you.*"

"I'm fine," John said sharply, looking away from Willy's concerned face. "I've never been better."

"You look like shit!" Willy cried, startling John with her intensity and crudeness. "Look at yourself, John! You must have lost fifteen pounds in the past month—your clothes just *hang* on you! And your color is awful, you look ill, your complexion is almost gray—"

"It's winter, Willy," John protested. "I've been working hard."

"John, you look exhausted and underweight and ill," Willy said. "You look *haunted.*"

John let his eyes meet Willy's. For a few moments something opened inside him, and their old connection sparked between them. Once John had believed he and Willy were among the lucky few who were truly well married, who belonged to each other. Now he sensed that this was still so; they still belonged to each other, and for these few moments while he chafed against the knowledge, he also felt safe in it, was glad for the security of it, in the way a man is glad, after all, to be some mother's child.

He almost thought that he could tell Willy the whole truth and she would not fly in a rage at him, but would instead understand and help him.

He caught himself in the very middle of the thought. What

did he mean, Willy would help him? How on earth could Willy help him?

He just wanted Willy to go away, that was all. He just wanted Willy to leave him alone. He looked away from Willy.

"I know what you want," Willy said quietly.

John did not look up. His scorn for his wife, his impatience with her, was flooding back into him.

"You want me to leave you alone, don't you?" Willy said. Her voice was calm and low. "You want me to go away and leave you in peace with—with your paintings and your *ghost.* Am I right?"

Still John did not look up. He felt guilty, and angry at Willy for this. At the same time, he was slightly surprised at how well she knew his mind. What else did she know about him?

"Well, I'll do it," Willy went on. She was toying with a silver spoon, turning it over and over against the tablecloth. "I'll leave you alone for a while. I'm going to go to Boston. The carpenters are through here. Anne's baby is due any day now. I'll stay with the Hunters and help them with the baby."

John's heart leaped up at her words. The freedom—! He did not dare let her know how he wanted it. He did not look at his wife.

"You see how much I love you, John," Willy was saying. "How enormous and complete my love for you is. I can give you this, I can go away, because I love you and I know you and I can sense what it is you need now. I'll leave in the morning. I'll be gone two or three weeks. I'll—"

Willy continued talking, but John did not hear her. He let her words flow over and around him, like water that cannot move a heavy stone.

When Willy said, "John, will you sleep with me tonight? Make love to me tonight? Before I leave?" John still did not look up, did not answer. He remained seated at the table, looking down at his hands. He felt Willy's sadness, her tears, how he had hurt her, as she walked around the dining room, blowing out the candles. He felt her sorrow as a stone feels the plaintive sob and drag of the sea, and he had no help for her, no more than a stone had for the water surging helplessly past.

Finally, Willy went to bed. He heard the bed creak as she settled in. He rose and went to the attic where Jesse Orsa was waiting for him, her young smooth skin warm, so warm, to his touch.

FOR A WHILE IN BOSTON, WILLY WAS MERCIFULLY TOO BUSY TO THINK much about John. The day after she arrived, Anne went into a long and exhausting and complicated labor. Willy sat with Anne while Mark ran out for a quick meal. Willy held Anne's hands, put a washcloth filled with ice to her friend's parched lips, rubbed Anne's back.

"I wish Mark weren't so gung ho on this natural-childbirth shit," Anne panted. "I want to curse and scream and bitch and yell, and I can't with him around. It would worry him too much."

Willy laughed. She was sorry her friend was in pain, yet she was so happy to be with her, to be back in Boston, to be around friends who knew and loved her. And finally the baby was born, a large, healthy boy with Mark's blond hair.

"Look at him! He's gorgeous!" Willy laughed when the nurse let her hold the baby, who was named Peter after his grandfather. "What a gorgeous, lovely brand-new person he is, Annie. God, it really is a miracle, isn't it?"

Anne and Mark were gooney with love and pride.

Willy did what she could to help when the baby came home; she cooked the dinners and cleaned the apartment and did the laundry. But mostly during the day the baby and Anne slept, and at night both parents got up to change and feed and rock and adore their new child. They talked about the baby obsessively those first few days; the world could have fallen down around them without arousing their interest. So Willy had time on her hands.

For a week she spent her time having lunch or dinner with friends, seeing movies, wandering through her favorite museums, visiting the stores that sold her embroidered work. She called John once; he was pleasant but lukewarm, distant, unenthusiastic. Even, she thought, weak. He sounded weak to her. But she said nothing about this to him.

Still, the next day she decided she had to do something. To at least try.

Armed with ads circled in local newspapers, she went first of all to see A. Gardner Borgiss, doctor of parapsychology. He had a small but elegant apartment on Beacon Hill and saw clients in his book-lined study, where he offered a choice of sherry or Perrier. Dr. Borgiss was a fat man who seemed very happy with life; his eyes twinkled behind thick bifocals. He tugged at his salt-and-pepper beard as he listened to Willy talk. Then, for over an hour, he asked what Willy thought were good and intelligent questions. But when their session was over, his theory was very much like George Glidden's: John's mind was playing tricks on him because of his need to prove himself as an artist.

"Let him go on this way," Dr. Borgiss said. "Then someday, soon, I'm sure, he will exhibit his work in a gallery. When he goes public with it—comes out of the closet, so to speak—his 'ghost' will disappear. You can count on it."

This session cost her one hundred dollars.

Next she went to a woman who advertised her services as a psychic. This skinny, nervous, rather unclean woman wore a tweed skirt and a stretched-out and shabby cardigan and looked relieved when Willy refused her offer of tea. They sat across from each other on a threadbare sofa in her tiny apartment. The woman began to tell Willy about Willy's past and her loved ones, and the information was so ridiculously wrong, so far from the truth, that Willy almost burst out laughing. But she was afraid for the woman's sanity, afraid that if she just walked out, the woman might have a fit or something. So she sat through the poor creature's spiel and left the thirty dollars she asked for.

Finally, the third day of searching, Willy found a medium who listened to Willy's tale with sympathy and agreed to give her a séance. "Perhaps my contact can find out something about this ghost for you," she said.

This woman was plump but attractive, a sort of brunette Zsa-Zsa Gabor, not without a greal deal of charm. She had a large old house in Cambridge furnished with magnificent and ornate antiques. While several beautifully groomed cats roamed around the large room, which was darkened by heavy draperies against the late-morning light, Mellicent Mogliana closed her eyes and bent her hands to a heavy walnut table. The room was sweet with incense, and very warm, and Willy found herself impressed with the atmosphere the woman created. She could almost believe that the woman had gone into a trance, was speaking to a mischievous creature named "Teddy." And when Teddy had no help to give, Willy found herself bursting into tears.

She sat next to the heavy old table and sobbed, unable to stop. Mellicent Mogliana pressed a button on the floor that brought a servant with a silver tray of tea. She poured some for Willy and insisted she drink it. She had the servant open the drapes.

"Tell me more," she ordered Willy. "Tell me everything."

So Willy told her everything, not just that there was a ghost in the house, a female, whom only her husband could see, who visited only her husband, but that she knew her husband was having an affair with this ghost. That her husband had been losing weight, not eating, not making love to Willy, not spending any time with her, spending all his time in the attic. That she knew her husband was in love with the ghost.

The medium rose from her chair and came to stand

by Willy. She placed her heavily jeweled hands on Willy's shoulders.

"Look at me," she said. "Listen to me, my daughter, my sister. I know many things. I have heard and seen and learned many things. And you must believe me. You must not trouble yourself so. It is possible, very possible, that your husband is in some kind of contact with a spirit—a ghost, if you will. It is possible that she speaks to him, perhaps even that he sees her. But only briefly, only for a very short while. It is not possible that he could be, as you put it, having an affair with her. That is not possible. Spirits can do some certain things. They can move physical things, cause physical things to move. They can make sounds and make themselves seen. But my daughter, my sister, trust me, they cannot have back their sensate bodies. Ah, if only they could! No, your husband is not having an affair with a ghost. Such a thing is not possible. Please believe me and put your mind at rest."

Willy paid the woman seventy-five dollars for her time and advice and went away, still troubled.

Today was one of February's silver days, when the sun shone through layers of snow-filled clouds. By night a heavy snow would be falling; today the air was filled with dispersed radiance and a cold shimmering. It was early afternoon.

Willy walked listlessly through Harvard Square, oblivious to the bustle of people and cars, unaware of the shops filled with chocolates and flowers and books. She did not want to go back to the Hunters' apartment just yet. The atmosphere there was so thick with baby these days; if little Peter was asleep, she would have to tiptoe and whisper and listen to Anne describe in detail what he did all morning; if he was awake, she would have to either sit and adore him or run little frantic errands around the house for Anne, fetching another diaper or the pacifier or the baby powder. And always Anne's face would be ecstatic, for Anne was consumed, possessed, with love for her child. Willy was glad for Anne but troubled for herself. It was not that she was jealous of the baby. It was that she needed someone to talk to. She needed some help and did not know where on earth to find it.

She walked along down Brattle Street, and without planning it, she found herself at Mt. Auburn Cemetery. The high gates were open; she wandered in and strolled along the winding paths, looking at the ornate and elegant stone monuments. She saw no one else, not even the groundskeeper's truck. It was very quiet and peaceful, as it was meant to be, and yet the trees stretched their bare brown arms into the sky triumphantly, wordlessly proclaiming, even in the dead of winter, the vivid life that lay hushed and waiting within.

Willy loved this cemetery. She and John had come here often when they were first lovers. They had strolled arm in arm among the graves, reading off the epitaphs, exclaiming about the beauty of the flowers and bushes and carved marble. How many times had they stood on the tower at the top of the hill, leaning against each other, looking down over the gently rolling landscape of Cambridge and Boston, at the curving Charles River. They had felt united then, at the apex of time and space.

And now she was here alone. Willy realized that it was the first time she had been here alone. And she was so lonely. She could make no sense out of what was happening to her life. She could no longer pretend that something wasn't wrong. But where could she find help? Her best friends were preoccupied with their baby; the professionals of this enlightened city had had no wisdom to offer her, or at least no solace, no helpful advice; she had no family to turn to. The women she had met in Nantucket were pleasant, but they were also busy with their own lives, and she had not become intimate with any of them yet. Not intimate enough to confess to any one of them that she was afraid her husband was having an affair with a ghost.

A ghost.

Willy sank onto the ground in a spot where the grass was

thick and bent over with its weight. She did not shiver, did not feel the need to remain alert or on guard. She sat surrounded by graves, tombstones, memorials to the dead, and yet in this place she had no feeling of ghostliness. Here she was not afraid or intrigued; she had absolutely no sensation of spirits moving around her. Perhaps it was that she was just an extraordinarily dull person. An insensitive person. A realistic, practical *clod* of a person with no romance in her soul.

Willy bent her head and wept.

When she finally rose, she was cramped and cold and tired, and she was not refreshed. She still did not know what to do.

IT WAS ONLY HER SENSE OF HAVING STAYED TOO LONG AT THE Hunters' that made Willy rouse herself to go back to Nantucket. She had been with Anne and Mark for almost three weeks, and Anne's mother and father were due to arrive in a few days to stay with them and see the baby. Willy knew her presence was becoming intrusive. Her friends needed some time to have their home to themselves before their relatives came. So, in spite of their protests, she packed up and headed home.

She had managed, the last day of her stay, to do one thing for herself. She had gotten herself a cat. The pet store in Cambridge had been crowded with new kittens of all colors that were either piteously mewing or cunningly pushing their paws through the wire of their cage to play. But Willy had chosen an older animal, a cat that was almost a year old, because this cat had been sitting in her cage so calmly, queening it over all the others, clearly too proud to beg. She was a large, long-haired, tabby-colored cat with a white ruff and white feet and a dainty pink nose that Willy fancied the cat was vain about. She had such an aura of knowingness about her, this cat, and when she deigned to meet Willy's eyes, her look was not that of an animal supplicating a higher being but rather of one equal looking at another. Willy named the cat Aimee, after the French for friend, and thought perhaps she had found an intimate in this cat.

She would let the cat sleep on the bed, she decided. Then she would not—perhaps—miss quite so much the warmth and weight of John's body when he spent his nights in the attic.

She took the last ferry that left Hyannis at nine and would get into Nantucket around midnight. She had not called John to tell him that she would be coming home. Now, as she sat on the ferry, staring out through the glass at the black water, black sky, listening to the steady churn of the engines of this calm and uncaring machine that carried her so thoughtlessly over unimaginable depths, she wondered about her motives. Had she neglected to call John because she didn't want to disturb him or because subconsciously she hoped to surprise him, *catch* him at something? At what? What was it she was worried about? What could she be thinking of? She knew his deepest secrets, she knew even what had embarrassed him when he was sixteen years old. She knew where to touch him sexually to please him. Still, he was a stranger to her now, and this simple act of returning home unannounced was filling her with an unexpected tension and a mysterious sense of guilt.

The house was dark. This did not surprise her; it was late, after all. She had thought that she would be overcome with curiosity and tenderness at the sight of her new cat, her new friend, cautiously investigating the house, for cats were like humans, individual in their reactions and responses. She turned on a few lights as she walked through the house and ended in the kitchen, where she opened the refrigerator, intending to set out some milk in a saucer for Aimee to drink.

But the sight—and smell—of the kitchen took her thoughts entirely away from the cat. The rancid odor that exploded outward at her when she opened the refrigerator door made her gasp. She stood there, holding the door open, amazed, slowly realizing that everything in the refrigerator had been there over three weeks ago when she had left Nantucket for Boston. The thickened milk clung to the sides of its clear plastic carton. Shriveled lettuce and vegetables, mildewed zucchini and mucousy green peppers lay moistly decaying in the vegetable bin. Willy shut the door and looked around at the rest of the kitchen.

Her coffee cup from three weeks ago still sat in the sink where she had left it, scum growing on the surface of the dregs. There were no other dirty dishes; either John had washed them all, or he had used no dishes during the past three weeks. Cartons of crackers sat opened on the counters, the paper torn and crumbled. At least eight mugs of half-drunk coffee sat on every available space, leaving brown rings on the table, the stove, the countertops.

Perhaps it was just the normal mess of temporary bachelorhood, and yet there was something just enough wrong with it all to send Willy racing out of the kitchen and up the stairs.

Their bedroom was dark. She had made the bed the morning she left, and it was still made, as chaste and unrumpled as she had left it. Would John leave the kitchen in such chaos and still trouble to make the bed so perfectly? She didn't think so.

"John?" she called, but not loudly, as if she were almost afraid of his reply.

"Oh, God," she said quietly, standing in her bedroom and the words really were a prayer.

Then she started slowly down the hall to the door to the attic.

The light was on. She climbed the stairs deliberately, not trying to hush the sounds of her steps but not calling out. Her heart was thudding in her chest.

The attic was very cold. Ice grew in elaborate, fantastical patterns on the inside of the windows; it was as if leaves were etched in the white frost. That was what she first noticed—the cold.

Then she saw the pictures. He had finished perhaps ten of them, and they were all large, at least nine by nine, set all around the attic on the floor, leaning against the walls. And they were all the same pictures, or at first they seemed to be—they were pictures of shadows, executed in shades of gray and black. They were abstracts; that was the kindest thing that could be said about them. The black or gray was fanned onto the canvas and blurred to the edges, and if there was a depth anywhere, it was the depth of the conical interior of lilies, a beckoning depth that pulled one in.

She did not like these pictures. They were ugly. And frightening.

Then she saw John. He was collapsed on his bed at the other end of the attic, so deeply asleep that her arrival did not awaken him. She walked across to him, her winter boots sounding heavily against the wooden floor. She stood above him, looking down, looking at her sleeping husband, the man she loved.

He looked filthy. That was what she first noticed—that and the smell. He stank. Of sweat, of exhaustion, of coffee and alcohol—and of illness. His clothes were stained and wrinkled and dirty and mussed, he had not shaved for so long that a beard and mustache had grown to at least an inch's length on his face, and his hair was oily from lack of washing. She had never seen him look like this before, not even when he had been sick for several weeks with a debilitating flu. The sheets and quilt of the bed were twisted and rumpled, and soiled.

That was the kick in the stomach, the terrible, swift blow that made her bring her hands to her waist in an attitude of defense: the sight of those soiled sheets.

Once she had heard Mark and John laughing together about college days when a friend had arranged to rent a pornographic movie for a stag party. He had borrowed a projector from the university library but had used one of his own sheets off his bed for the screen. "God, his sheets were worse than the movie!" Mark and John had laughed.

Now Willy stood looking down at her filthy husband sprawled on his soiled, stained sheets, and tears came into her eyes. She was shaking, too, because of the extreme cold of the attic.

"Dear God," she whispered. "What's been going on?"

She knelt by the bed and took her husband's face in her hands. "John," she whispered. "John. Wake up. It's me. It's Willy. I'm home. Wake up." She shook him slightly; she caressed his face.

At last his eyes opened. He seemed drugged. He looked right at Willy and said, without any kind of preface, after all their three weeks apart, "I'm tired. Let me sleep. Please let me sleep." Then he closed his eyes.

"John!" Willy protested. She gently shook his shoulders. "Hey, *John*, come on!"

He opened his eyes again. "I need to sleep," he repeated.

But Willy was firm. "Then you can sleep downstairs. With me. After you've had a shower," she added. When he closed his eyes and turned his head away, she said, more loudly, "I mean it, John. I'm not leaving you up here in this cold alone. My God, what have you been doing? What's been going on?"

One more time John opened his eyes. He looked at Willy long enough for her to understand that he was conscious now and that he was aware of what he was saying.

"Willy," he said. "Go away. I want you to leave me alone." His voice was firm. His look was firm.

The hurt plunged through her so fiercely that it was as if it were her own body that had plunged through some cold, scraping element. She recoiled in disbelief.

But they had been married for so long, and something in her now came to his defense more powerfully than to her own. Even as she felt her body flinch backward from his words, she felt something else within her rise to steel her intentions and steady her voice. She gazed back at him with a look so calm it was almost a glare.

"No," she said, her voice quiet but deliberate. "No, John, I won't go away. I won't leave you alone up here. I want you to come downstairs with me."

He closed his eyes and turned his head away. He lay there, ignoring her.

Willy looked at her husband, feeling her chest expand with pain and frustration and anger and fear. And with cunning, for she heard herself saying, "All right, then, *I'll* get in bed with *you.*" And she rose and began to take off her clothes.

"No," John said, twisting on the bed to look at her. "Stop, Willy. You can't sleep here."

She was shaking now, from the cold, from fear, from anger. She didn't reply but kept on undressing.

"God damn it!" John said, and pushed himself up off the bed. "All right," he said. "Let's go. Come on. I'll go downstairs."

Willy gathered up her clothes; she had stripped down to her corduroy trousers and bra. She followed her husband down to the second floor, sighing in relief.

He went into the bathroom. Willy followed, her clothes in her hands, and leaned against the doorframe, watching him. When he turned, she said, "This is a lovely homecoming, I must say, John."

John looked at his wife. He ran his hand through his hair. He seemed completely exhausted.

"I'm sorry," he said without seeming to mean it. "I'm just so tired, Willy. I must have the flu."

"You must," Willy agreed. "You look like a fucking cadaver."

This made John burst into an abrupt bark of laughter. "A fucking cadaver!" he echoed. Then he edged his way past Willy out of the bathroom and headed to the guest bedroom. "I've got to get some rest, Willy," he said. "I'm exhausted."

"John," Willy protested, "wait a minute! You can't go to sleep now, not yet! I haven't seen you for three weeks. And look at you—you've lost so much weight. You look horrible. You've got to tell me what's been going on!"

"Tomorrow," John said, falling onto the twin bed.

"No, *now*!" Willy demanded. "John, why are you sleeping in the guest bedroom? Why won't you sleep with me?"

But John did not answer. He turned on his side and, without pulling up any covers, closed his eyes and fell asleep. Watching, Willy was alarmed at how fast her husband fell asleep. She sat down on the twin bed across from him and just looked at her husband for a while. She had never seen him looking so awful. He had never seemed so distant—so cruel; he had never hurt her so much.

And that part of her that was wounded cried out for extreme and dramatic reactions now; she wanted to cry and scream and wake John up and yell at him and hit him and throw things against the walls. "Go away," he had said to her, his voice as cold as ice. And he had not wanted her in that dreadful bed in the attic. She wanted to rage with jealousy and anger.

Yet something stronger within her again came to John's defense, and she was not as jealous as she was afraid, afraid for John's sake.

Aimee strolled into the room and, seeing Willy, sat just inside the doorway and meowed.

"Oh, poor kitty." Willy laughed, glad to see the cat. "I've forgotten all about you. Here. Come here. Come up with me."

With the cat curled up next to her, purring and warm, Willy began to relax. She could not puzzle this all out tonight. She had to talk to John; she had to get him to talk to her. But that would have to wait until morning. Still—still she did not want to leave his side, and so she did not rise to unpack her bag or change into a nightgown, but only snuggled under the covers and fell asleep on the guest-room bed, her cat next to her, her husband across from her, sleeping his fathomless sleep.

CHAPTER EIGHT

WHEN WILLY AWAKENED THE NEXT MORNING, SHE NOTICED first that John was still asleep and then that Aimee was still next to her, curled in a ball at the bend of her knees. She lay for a while appreciating the way the weak winter sun shone through the windows, filling this small room with a glazy light. Stretching, she looked at her wristwatch and was amazed to see that it was almost eleven o'clock. She glanced back over at John, alarmed—how could he still be sleeping so deeply?

Sitting up in bed, she pondered what to do next. Should she leave him alone to sleep? He had finished so many canvases; it was possible that he had pushed himself to the point of exhaustion. It was possible that it was only that that had happened while she was gone. But she did not think so. Yet she had no proof, only her suspicions and the memory of his voice and face as he told her to go away.

For a while, petulant, she decided she would damn well stay by his side for every minute of this day. But after she had settled back down into the bed, she grew restless. She never had been good at staying in bed all day. So she rose and showered and dressed, coming in now and then to check on John, who still slept.

Several times she walked past her sewing room, but it did not lure her now. All her thoughts were intent on one thing: What could she do to get John back to normal again? How could she get him to love her—to look at her, talk to her, touch her, confide in her, to be her lover, her friend, as he had always been? How could she win him back from whatever strange mood it was that had overtaken him?

She decided to seduce him. She never had enjoyed nagging—never had had to do much of it—and she did not look forward to a day filled with scenes and questions and recriminations. Better to lure him, to seduce him, to win him back to her side with love and little luxuries.

So while he slept in the guest room for the greater part of the day—and she kept checking, and still he slept—she hummed in the kitchen, determined, cleaning up the debris of the past three weeks and filling it with the aromas of foods John loved best: her homemade wholewheat bread, beef stew in Burgundy, apple cinnamon pie.

But she discovered that in the late afternoon, when she went out to buy fresh flowers to arrange around the house, John had awakened and gone up to the attic without touching anything in the kitchen, without fixing himself so much as a cup of coffee.

"John?" she called up from the bottom of the attic stairs. "Aren't you hungry?"

"I'm painting, Willy," was his only response.

Brazen now, Willy went uninvited up the attic stairs to see exactly what it was her husband was up to. And he was, in fact, painting, another dreary, dark, disturbing canvas. Willy stood at the top of the stairs, watching for a while. John was completely engrossed, sweeping the paint on in swirling motions, seemingly unaware of Willy's presence.

Willy took advantage of this to look around the attic. No other person was there—had she really expected someone would be? Had she expected some gorgeous ghost to be hovering just over John's left shoulder, inspiring him as he worked?

"I'm surprised the paint works in this cold," Willy said. "I'm surprised *you* can work in this cold."

He was silent so long she thought he was not going to answer, but finally he said, in a low voice, "The heaters are turned on. It just takes a while for the room to warm up."

He kept on painting, absorbed, until at last Willy turned and went down the stairs.

She walked through the lovely old house, thinking. Already the light was fading from the sky, and the rooms were filled with shadows. It was almost six o'clock; she wished John would come down to eat. The food smelled heavenly—how could he resist?

By seven he still had not come down, but she would not give up. There were other ways to seduce him.

She went to the bedroom and took out her sexiest nightgown, the red satin one that clung and dipped in just the right places. She brushed her hair out so that it hung shimmering down her back and over her shoulders. She applied what little makeup she owned—some lipstick and blush—and perfume. Finally, after scrutinizing herself in the mirror—her breasts were so exposed in this gown!—she went slowly up the stairs to the attic.

John was in the process of cleaning his brushes. He did not turn when Willy came to his side. So she moved behind him and leaned up against his back. She wrapped her arms around his waist and began to nuzzle and lightly kiss the back of his neck, the back of his ears, while at the same time running her hands up and down the front of his body.

"Through with work for the day?" she purred.

146

John pulled away from her. "Willy," he began.

She let him pull away. She stepped back so that he could get a good look at her. Then, because he only stood looking at her without speaking or moving, she took his hands and placed them on her breasts. She smiled at him and moved her head slowly so that her hair slid forward over his hand.

"Don't, Willy," John said, trying to pull his hands away.

"Don't what?" she asked, smiling, moving closer to him. "Why not? I'm your wife."

When he jerked his hands away in response, she moved even closer and put her arms up around his neck. "I think you've been working too hard," she said. "I think you need a little . . . rest and relaxation."

She kissed his neck, his face, his mouth, while moving her hands down his shoulders and over his body. It had been a long time since she had been so close to him physically, and she found herself becoming aroused by her actions. She wanted him. At some point she stopped operating, stopped manipulating, and let the instinctive need in her take over. She ground her body against his in little pushing movements.

And she felt him respond. Her breath came out in a jagged sigh, a mixture of relief and desire. When he began to kiss her back, to hold her to him, tears came into her eyes.

"Come," she whispered, and pulled him to the bed that lay waiting, rumpled, in the corner of the attic.

"No, Willy," John said, resisting, but at last he let himself be led to the bed, where they fell, husband and wife, together.

Willy was the assertive one. She rose above her husband, letting the strap of her gown fall down one shoulder so that most of one breast was exposed, and began to unbutton John's shirt, kissing his chest as she worked. She unzipped his pants.

But although he had been erect when they were standing on the other side of the attic, his body now would display no sign of interest. No matter what she did with her hands and

147

mouth, he stayed limp. Willy looked at her husband, who lay with his arms crossed over his face in an attitude of surrender.

"John?" she asked softly.

"It won't work, Willy," he said. "I can't."

"Lift up your hips so I can get your jeans off," Willy said.

Without speaking, John did as she said. As Willy tugged, she felt a movement behind her and, turning to look, saw that Aimee had come up the stairs and, after sniffing at the edge, had jumped up onto the bed. The cat sat at the end of the bed, watching the humans, purring her approval.

Willy removed John's jeans and undershorts. She took off her gown. Finally, they were naked together, after so many weeks apart. She lay down on top of him, nuzzling her head against his shoulder, subtly moving her hips against his.

"It's all right," she said. "You're tired, you're exhausted, you've been working so hard, and you've got to be hungry." She began to kiss him softly as she spoke, licking here and there. "It's good just to be together like this, isn't it?" she said. "It's been so long since we've been together; you've forgotten how it is for us, haven't you? Oh, Johnny, I love you, sweet man," she said, and she felt his body responding. She smiled, secretly triumphant.

She pushed herself up in order to move him inside her. He had moved his arms now so that his hands were on her breasts, and he lay looking at her with an expression she could not read. Just as she lifted her hips so that he could enter her, a sound tore the air next to them, startling Willy.

"Wrrrooow!"

The cat's cry was piercing, high, and frightening.

Willy looked around and saw that Aimee, still on the foot of the bed, was standing now, her back arched, her fur ruffled and erect. The cat was slowly walking backward, snarling, her entire body bristling with fear.

"Aimee?" Willy said softly. She reached out her hand.

But the cat paid no attention to Willy. It continued to carefully back away from something, making hissing and snarling noises as it did.

Willy scanned the attic, but she could not see what the cat was frightened of. She became aware of intense cold in the air and then of the way John's body shrunk away from hers.

"Johnny?" she asked, turning to look back at her husband.

"She's my WIFE!" John shouted.

Willy whipped her head around to see the person John was addressing, but no one was there. And still Aimee slunk backward on the bed, her fur ruffled, her teeth bared.

Someone else was in the room with them. Willy could sense her presence now even though she could see nothing. She moved off John's body and reached for her gown, wrapping it around her torso, towel fashion, to hide her nakedness.

"Who are you?" she called into the air. "What are you doing here? What do you want?"

She looked around her for some sign, some movement, and was startled to find herself being grabbed by her husband. John sat up in bed and grasped Willy's arms in his hands.

"Do you see her?" he asked, nearly shouting. "Do you see her?"

"No," Willy replied, "but I feel her. I know she's there, John."

In response, John buried his face in his hands. "Oh, God," he sobbed. "Don't you see, now, Willy?" he asked. "It's all over. It's decided. I'm hers now. This house is hers, and I am hers."

"No," Willy protested. "No, Johnny. No." She leaned over to comfort him, but he drew away from her touch.

"Please," he said. "Please just leave me alone."

Willy knelt on the bed next to her naked husband, who now had turned on his side, his back to her, his face hidden in his hands. Miserable and baffled, she just stayed like that awhile, holding her red satin gown around her body, wondering what to do. Aimee had calmed down now and came to settle next to John, her feet tucked under her and her fur settled but her eyes still wary. Willy was grateful for the cat's company; she felt lonelier than she had ever felt in her life. She did not have any idea how she would comfort her husband. When she reached out to touch his shoulder, he flinched away from her as if her touch burned.

"I need to sleep, Willy," John said. "I have to sleep."

"My God, how can you sleep now?" Willy protested. "John, we have to talk. I don't understand what's happening."

He did not respond. Frustrated, Willy sank down into a sitting position on the bed and pulled her gown over her head so that it was properly on her now. It did little to warm her against the cold of the attic. She could feel that the crisis had somehow passed: The cat was calm, the air was calm, John was relaxed. In fact, John was, she realized with surprise, sound asleep. Just like that, he had fallen into a deep sleep.

Willy looked at her sleeping husband, feeling exasperated, baffled, and deeply afraid. She didn't know what to do. She sat there for almost an hour, watching John sleep, waiting for something else to happen, waiting to feel something in the air, wondering what on earth she should do. Her thoughts were racing, but gradually her pulse slowed, for the room remained silent except for John's breathing and the cat's little noises.

Willy's back began to ache. She stretched, and the cat, in response, looked up at her and mewed.

"I know, I know, you're hungry," Willy said to the cat. "And the stew has probably burned on the bottom of the pot by now. And I'm freezing. I could use a nice stiff drink." She picked the cat up and held it in her arms. "Come on," she said. "Let's go downstairs."

She bent over and pulled the soiled comforter up over her husband's naked body. He looked so frail to her; he had lost so much weight; and in his nakedness he seemed vulnerable. Willy stood a moment looking around the attic. If anything was there, she could not sense it.

At any rate, she reminded herself wryly, the ghost would not hurt John. John had said he belonged to her. Surely she would not hurt him while he slept.

At the top of the stairs, she stopped, turned, and looked around her again. The attic was bright with fluorescent lights, cold, and quiet except for the even sounds of John's deep breathing as he slept.

"It's not true, you know," Willy said aloud, speaking to whomever might be there. "This is *not* your house. This is *our* house, Johnny's and mine. And he is *my* husband."

She waited, half expecting a response, but nothing moved, all was still. Cradling the cat against her breast, Willy went down the stairs.

~~~~~~~

BUT SHE COULD NOT RELAX. SHE COULD NOT CALM DOWN. THE thought that something, someone, whatever or whoever she was, was up there now with John, was in their house, filled her with tension. No matter how she replayed in her mind the events of the past few hours, she could make no sense out of it. She felt hysteria rising in her like a filling well.

In her bedroom, she pulled off the satin gown, letting it drop to the floor, and stepped into her favorite old robe, a thick satin-lined heavy green wool. She felt protected in it. She yanked her hair back into a long ponytail and roughly fastened it with a band, then turned and went down into the kitchen. Aimee followed her, rubbing against her legs.

While Aimee ate the dinner Willy set out for her, Willy leaned against the kitchen counter, drinking a vodka and tonic and eating beef stew. She ate so fast she burned her tongue and could not taste the food, but her eating was only a frantic way of fortifying herself. In the midst of a bite she gagged and spit the mouthful back into the bowl. She put the bowl in the sink.

"This is horrible, horrible!" she cried out, pressing her hands to her temples. "What are we going to do?"

"Be calm, Willy, be calm," she answered herself, but that was of little help.

She took up the kitchen phone and dialed the Hunters' number. Mark answered.

"God, Willy, you left just in time," he said. "We've all come down with a monster flu today."

"Mark," Willy said, taking deep breaths so that she would not sound hysterical, "listen to me. I need your help desperately. You've got to come here. You've got to see John. He's in trouble. We're in trouble."

"What's wrong?" Mark asked.

"It's the ghost—" Willy began, but Mark interrupted.

"Willy," he said, chiding. "Come on."

"Listen to me!" Willy exclaimed. "I know you don't believe it. I didn't, either, but it's true. Oh, Mark, you've got to come here. You've got to help us. Please."

"Willy, I just told you. I can't come. Anne and I are both flat on our backs with this damned flu. Actually, it would be better if we were flat on our backs. Most of the time we're bent over the toilet, puking. We can hardly take care of Peter."

In response, Willy began to sob into the telephone. "I'm so afraid," she said. "Mark, I'm so afraid."

"Now calm down, Willy," Mark said, alarm in his voice. "Look, tell me what's been going on. Explain it to me."

Willy took a deep breath. "When I got home," she said, "I found the attic in a horrid mess. And John was filthy. He hadn't shaved or bathed or—"

"Had he been painting?" Mark asked.

"Yes. Yes, horrid, bleak stuff."

"Well, then," Mark replied. "Maybe you don't care for it,

but the fact is he was working while you were gone. Probably got so involved in his work he didn't care about shaving or bathing. That's hardly anything to get worried about, Willy. You know we men need you females around to keep us up to mark in the cleanliness department. Not to seem sexist—"

"It's more than that!" Willy said. "John's lost so much weight. He looks terrible. He looks skinny and weak and pale and awful!"

"He's probably had the flu," Mark said. "Really, Willy, if you could see us, you'd say the same thing about us. Right after you left, we started throwing up, and we've been doing it every hour on the hour. We're both dehydrated and drawn looking and have black circles under our eyes—"

"He won't sleep with me!" Willy interrupted, nearly shouting. "I can't get him interested in me sexually."

Mark was quiet a minute, surprised at this intimate detail. "Well, Willy," he said, "if he's been sick, the way we've been sick, I wouldn't worry. The last thing we're interested in now is sex, believe me. We couldn't find the energy for it to save our lives."

"But he doesn't have the flu," Willy protested. "He's involved with a ghost. Don't laugh, Mark, listen to me, I know it's true. She was up in the attic with us."

"Did you see her?"

"No," Willy replied. "But—but I sensed her. And the cat walked backwards with her fur ruffled up, hissing and snarling. The cat saw her."

Mark was quiet again. "You think there was a ghost in the attic because your cat walked backwards?" he said, his voice even.

"Oh, damn you," Willy cried. "Why won't you believe me? Why would I want to make up something like this? Mark, you know me. I'm not the type to go around seeing things. Why can't you believe me?"

"What's John doing now?" Mark asked.

"He's asleep. In the attic. On that soiled bed. He's naked. That's another thing—he sleeps all the time. And I can't get him to eat. He just sleeps. He falls asleep so easily and sleeps so much!"

Mark took a deep breath and let it out in a long sigh. "Willy," he said, "I hate to say this, but I feel like shit. I'm going to have to hang up and get to the bathroom in a minute; I'm sorry, but it can't be helped. Listen, honey, it sounds to me like John has got the same creeping crud we've got here. You're bound to get it yourself. Then you'll understand. When you're this sick, you can't eat, you don't want to eat, because you only upchuck everything, and all you want to do is sleep. You have to sleep. Now I'm sure that John has this flu. It's everywhere. Watch the evening news; they're talking about how many schoolchildren are absent these days because of it. It's a new strain, a new virus. I'm sure that's all that's wrong with John. Just give him a few days to recover, then he'll be your old John again. Come on, Willy, be sensible. There's no ghost in your attic, I don't care what your cat did. Cats get spooked easily, especially in new places. Just relax and let poor John sleep and I promise you in a few days he'll be eating and screwing like the old John again. All right?"

"All right," Willy said, giving up. What else could she say? Mark did not believe her; and she couldn't blame him. It was all preposterous.

She hung up the phone and leaned against the kitchen wall, feeling defeated.

IT WAS NOT EVEN NINE O'CLOCK YET. WILLY CLIMBED TO THE ATTIC and looked at John; he was still in a deep sleep. She sat on the end of the bed awhile, thinking. She went back downstairs and fixed herself a cup of hot chocolate, then stopped by their bedroom to pull on wool socks and a wool sweater over her robe. It was so cold in the attic she didn't know how John could stand it. But when she went back upstairs, he was asleep, oblivious to the cold.

What could she do? It seemed there was nothing she could do. Her husband had told her that he belonged to a ghost and would not make love to her, and she felt she had experienced a ghost—and yet there was nothing she could do. She could not understand how, after all that had happened this evening, John could so easily fall asleep, how he could stay asleep. Willy looked at him, feeling nearly insane with emotions. And John slept. She was wildly frustrated.

But she was not defeated. Not so easily defeated. She didn't know what was going on, she didn't know the rules, she didn't even know all the players of this game, but she had always been a good sport; she didn't give up easily. She wouldn't give up: she wouldn't give up her husband.

Willy made one more trip back down the stairs, Aimee accompanying her as she walked. She got a heavy comforter and a pillow and a thick book she had been wanting to read. Back in the attic, she made herself as comfortable as she could next to her sleeping husband. Then she opened her book and read, only half seeing the words on the pages. She was waiting for something to happen.

But nothing more happened that night, and at last Willy fell asleep, the book by her side, aware only of Aimee curled next to her and of the sound of her husband's even breaths.

~~~~~~~

THEY HAD MADE WILLY AN ASTRONAUT AND SENT HER UP IN THIS COLD metal ship that was so tiny that the walls pressed in on her body. She rolled this way and that, trying to avoid the intense cold that stung against her neck and arms and legs. She could not escape from the rigid freezing trap—and then suddenly she could, she had twisted away and broken out of the space capsule and was flung into the black void of space, which was even more chilling than the capsule had been. She tried to cry out "No!" but her voice was caught in her throat, and there was nothing she could do to avoid the endless, whirling, sickening fall through an air so black and dead and deficient of warmth that she felt her lips turning blue. She grabbed out with both hands to catch herself and found nothing. She tried to open her eyes but found them glued shut. She could feel her heart slowing in her body even as her thoughts raced in horror at her fall. She knew she was dying, and not even her terror could prevent it.

Then, with the most gentle and minute of thuds, she felt her body hit something. In all of infinite, bleak space, in the midst of the eternal emptiness, something was suddenly there, a nudge at her side, which brought her back to consciousness. Willy opened her eyes and looked down at the cat, which lay pressed against her thigh. The cat was awake. Even in the dark of the attic, Willy could make out the gleam of the cat's open eyes.

Taking deep breaths, Willy reached out and stroked Aimee. In return, the cat narrowed her eyes in a mute affectionate message. Aimee tucked her legs under her and purred but did not close her eyes or sleep.

Willy raised her arm to look at her watch. She had to push both her robe and sweater up her wrist to do so. It was only five-thirty. Her shoulders and back were cramped and rigid from hunching against the cold, and yet she could hear the occasional pings of the three oil radiators as they worked to warm the room, and she could tell now that it was not so very cold here—what a terrible freakish dream she had been having!

She wanted to wake John to tell him about her nightmare, for it had been so real; she felt that she actually had been falling through dark, cold space, and she was as frightened as a child and needed comforting badly.

"John?" she whispered. She nudged him. She nudged him again. "John?"

He did not respond. He lay next to her, so still, that suddenly panicked, Willy threw herself against him to listen for his breath and his heartbeats. He was still alive, only sunk in a profound sleep. Willy resigned herself to the comfort of his body against hers. She snuggled against him, hoping to relax against his warmth, but he felt strangely cool to her.

Dear God, she thought, what is happening to us? To him?

She lay awake then, alert, trying to *feel* anything—anyone that might enter the attic, trying to be aware of the slightest change in sound or temperature or shadow. She was aware of Aimee's presence, how the cat moved across the bed after Willy had moved so that once again the animal had settled down, just touching Willy. She could hear Aimee purr, and several times as she twisted uncomfortably on the bed, she noticed that the cat was not sleeping but just lying there, looking content but very much awake. This gave Willy immense comfort.

She lay there holding her husband, straining to be aware of the slightest change in atmosphere, until the faint light of early morning stained the windows and the rumblings of passing cars and trucks on Orange Street informed her that a new day had begun.

~~~~~~~~~

SHE LOOKED AT HER WATCH AGAIN. IT WAS SEVEN-THIRTY. SHE WAS exhausted and yet too disquieted to get back to sleep. While she had lain awake during the early morning, she had tried to think sensibly about the events of the past evening, but who could make sense out of such things? Now she was just as confused as ever.

Certain things were clear to her, though: She sensed a very

real danger here in the attic for herself and for John. It seemed very possible to her that she could lose him somehow; that she was losing him somehow. She would not concede that she had lost him yet.

She could not lie, cramped and cold and uncomfortable, in the bed any longer; she could not wait any longer to get things straight with John. So she rose, and being sure to shut the attic door tightly so the cat was shut in the attic—and feeling foolish as she did, thinking, Good, Willy, you leave that cat to protect John from a ghost, you're thinking clearly today—she went down to the kitchen. Working as quickly as she could, she made a large pot of coffee, scrambled eggs, and toast and carried it all on a tray back up to the attic.

John was still asleep.

"Good morning!" she called with a false heartiness. "Breakfast!"

But he was not to be roused so easily. She had to set the tray on the little mahogany table—pushing aside the small, elegant wineglasses—and go to the bed and shake John before he would wake up.

"Oh, Willy," John said when he opened his eyes. "Don't." His head fell back against the pillow.

Willy was insistent. At first she joked with him, saying teasing things, but finally she grew rough and adamant: "John, I am not going to let you sleep now. We have to talk. You have to wake up. Now come on." And she slapped his face.

With great weariness, John opened his eyes again and looked at his wife. "Let it go, Willy," he said.

"Get up. Come have breakfast. It's getting cold," Willy replied, her voice hard. She pulled on John's arms until he came up into a sitting position and then finally stood, his posture as rounded and stooping as a much older man's. He moved to the chair by the table with great reluctance and, once there, just sat until Willy insisted that he take a cup of coffee in his hand and drink. He would not look at Willy.

Husband and wife sat across from each other in the two brocade chairs, and Aimee padded across the thick carpet to sit at Willy's feet. She mewed lightly, and in response, Willy put some of her egg on a saucer and set it on the floor for the cat. She ate her own breakfast quickly; she was ravenous. She watched John; he sipped his coffee without interest. She was startled when he spoke.

"That's a nice cat," he said.

It was such a normal thing to say that Willy sighed with relief.

"Yes," she said. "Her name's Aimee. She's smart, I think, and very affectionate. She's stuck by my side ever since we got home."

"I was going to get you a cat, Willy," John said in the tone of voice of one who once remembered walking on the moon. "I really was." He took a sip of coffee and sat there as if deep in thought. After a while, he said, "For Christmas. I was going to get you a cat for Christmas. But there were no kittens available. I didn't think you'd want a grown cat."

Willy watched John carefully as he spoke. She had never seen him think so slowly before or with such effort. It seemed he actually had to work to remember when it was he had intended getting her a cat.

"John," she said quietly, leaning forward to get him to look at her, "we have to talk. I'm very worried about you. About us. About what's going on."

John looked at Willy for a long time. When he spoke, his voice was infinitely sad. "Oh, Willy," he said, "I loved you so much."

Alarmed at his use of the past tense and at his sorrow, Willy leaned farther and put her hand gently on his knee.

"John," she said quietly, "what do you mean, you *loved* me? Don't you love me anymore?"

In answer, John dropped his eyes. He shook his head slowly. "Not that way. Not the way I did."

"John—" Willy began, her voice sensible.

John raised his head and looked at Willy. "I love her," he said. His eyes were filled with tears. "God help me, I love her."

Willy pulled her hand away from her husband's knee and crossed both arms over her breasts, hugging herself for protection. The emotions that were surging through her were so powerful that she was afraid she would scream or hit, and so she rose and walked around the attic, holding herself tightly.

"Love *who*?" she demanded. "Who is *she*?" She was shaking so hard she could scarcely speak.

"You know," John said, looking directly at Willy. He looked ravaged with sorrow.

"A GHOST?" Willy yelled in spite of her good intentions. "Are you going to sit there and tell me you're in love with a ghost? Oh, John—"

John looked away from Willy. Softly, he said, "If I could change things . . ."

"Yes?" Willy challenged. "Go on. Finish your sentence. If you could change things, what? You would stop loving her and love me?" When he did not answer, she said, "Oh, John, really, this is preposterous! This is crazy! You've got to know it's crazy."

"I know that's what you think, and I don't blame you," John said. "But it's true, Willy. It has happened, and I can't go back now."

Willy stood shaking, the first hot, healthy surge of anger passing now and a chilling sweep of fear taking its place. She took deep breaths and forced herself to calm down. She walked back to her chair and sat.

"Can you tell me about it? About her?" she asked. When John didn't answer at once, she said, "I think I deserve to know something."

"Her name is Jesse Orsa Wright," John said. "She lived about a hundred and fifty years ago. In this house, I mean. Her husband built this house for her. He was the captain of a whaling ship—" John stopped. He looked up at Willy with a tortured expression. "Oh, God, Willy," he said. "I hate talking about her. I feel like I'm betraying her to talk about her."

"You feel like you're betraying *her*!" Willy said, her voice almost a shriek. "What do you feel like you're doing to me?"

John caved in, fell back against the chair, looked down at the floor. He was very pale. Willy sat, breathing hard, looking at him for a while.

"And she's a ghost," Willy went on finally, composed again, her voice low. "She's a ghost?"

"Yes," John said.

"But you can see her. And hear her. And—touch her," Willy prompted.

"Yes," John answered again.

"What does she look like?" Willy asked.

A slight smile crossed John's face in spite of himself; a smile of pleasure. "Willy—" he protested, catching himself.

"Please, John," Willy said. "Tell me." When he sat in silence for a moment, resisting, she added, "I won't freak out. I promise."

"She's small. Slim. She's . . . beautiful. She's young. Very young. Like a girl. She has very long dark hair and very large dark eyes, and her skin is as white as a gardenia petal." He looked up at Willy then to see her reaction.

Willy felt as though she had been stabbed. The thought of this girl who was as lovely as a gardenia petal—she thought of a gardenia, its fragrance and creaminess and luscious beauty. John had described the girl well enough. Willy felt her own body grow larger and more practical, like a sack, as she sat there imagining her husband's lover.

"I see," she said at last. "And—and she comes to you often?"

"Yes," John said.

"And you make love?" Willy asked, because she had to know.

161

"Yes," John said, his voice very low.

"She's really here, in the flesh, and you can feel her and see her and be touched by her—kiss her, all those things?" Willy pressed on in spite of her pain.

"Yes," John answered simply.

Willy made a little snorting sound as she tried to sniff back her tears. She tossed her head. "Well, is she *nice*?" she asked.

"That doesn't particularly come into it," John said.

Tears ran down Willy's face. "I mean, I mean, other than the physical, I mean, is she smart or interesting or clever or something?"

"She's clever," John said.

"Well, well, what do you *talk* about?" Willy demanded. "Does she tell you what it was like living here in the nineteenth century? Does she tell you that sort of thing?"

"We don't talk very much, Willy," John said softly.

And at that Willy buried her head in her hands and cried.

"I never meant to hurt you, Willy," John said, sounding helpless, lost. "I don't understand it. I don't know how it happened. I didn't *mean* for it to happen. It all seems—somehow beyond my control."

"But it's *not* beyond your control!" Willy declared, hope exploding within her at his apology.

"Willy—" John began.

"No, listen," Willy said, and wiped tears from her face with the front and back of her hands, "listen, John. It is in your control, I'm sure of it. *All you have to do is leave this house.*" She waited a moment, studying John's face, then pushed on: "Well? Am I right? Don't you think I'm right? All you have to do, John, is walk down the stairs and out of this house. I feel certain of that. She didn't bother us in Boston—I don't think she *can* go anywhere else. She has to have you here. That's why you're always in the attic—John, it *is* in your control! Just leave now. Just walk out of the house. Now. I'll go with you!"

Willy sat nearly panting, waiting for John's reaction.

He looked away from her. He said, so softly she could scarcely hear him, "I can't."

"You mean you don't want to," Willy snapped.

John was quiet for a long time. Then he lifted his head and looked at Willy defiantly. "That's right," he agreed. "I don't want to. Willy, I didn't mean for it to happen—I don't know how it happened—but I can't give her up. I'd rather give up my life."

"My God," Willy said, and the tears started up again.

They sat there awhile, husband and wife, wreathed and pierced with misery, and the coffee and food grew cold on the table between them. Willy cried. John leaned back against the chair, exhausted, and closed his eyes. His body went limp against the support of the chair. He was nearly asleep again when Willy spoke.

"Well, what are we going to do?" she asked.

"Do?" John echoed.

Willy broke out in a bitter, brief laugh. "I mean, do you want a divorce? I mean, shall I divorce you? I'll bet the courts don't have grounds for this sort of thing." When John didn't answer, she almost shouted, "Seriously, John, what are we going to do? Do you want me to move out? Are you going to spend the rest of your life up here in this goddamned attic? How are you going to carry on your . . . relationship . . . with this ghost of yours?"

John shook his head wearily, as if Willy had been browbeating him for hours and he could bear no more. He lifted his hand with great effort and brushed her suggestions aside. "I don't know, Willy," he said. "I don't know. You can go or stay, I guess. I—I really don't want much, I can't see too far ahead. There are some paintings I want to finish, and I want a few more days and nights in the attic, that's all."

"A few more days and nights in the attic—" Willy prompted, curious now, alerted by his words and the lethargy with which he spoke. "All right, and then what?"

"I don't know," John answered, irritated by her probing.

"Willy, I said I don't know much. Can't you just leave me alone? Just for a few more days and nights? That's all I ask."

Willy was calm now, and instincts other than jealousy were rising within her. She looked away from John and kept her voice level. "I'll make a deal with you," she said. "I'll keep away from you and the attic for *a few more days and nights*—for a week—if you'll agree to see a doctor today."

"I don't want to go out," John said.

"I'll get a doctor to come here," Willy said.

"I don't need a doctor!" John said.

"I think you do," Willy responded.

"I'm not crazy," John told her.

"I didn't say you were," Willy replied calmly. "I don't think you are. I think you're exhausted and weak and overworked and underweight, and maybe you've got a flu—it wouldn't hurt to have a doctor at least look at you."

"No," John said.

"You're afraid to have a doctor look at you!" Willy cried.

"Willy, I'm tired," John said. "That's all. I don't want to see a doctor. Forget it."

"Then I'm not leaving you alone," Willy said. "You can have your days and nights in the attic but not without me."

John raised his head and gave his wife a look of pure hatred.

"Why can't you just leave me alone?" he asked.

"I don't know," Willy replied honestly. "I don't know. But I can't. And I won't."

"Christ!" John muttered under his breath. He would have risen and stalked around the attic, but he was too weak; instead, he sat in his chair, his legs and arms shaking with anger and resentment.

While Aimee prowled into the corners of the attic, John and Willy sat across from each other, locked in fierce combat now, not speaking, each thinking his or her own thoughts.

Outside, it had begun to snow. The sky was as white as a

sheet, and great fluffy snowflakes fell gracefully, slowly, like icy feathers falling from an angel's ethereal wing.

Once again John was nearly asleep in his chair when Willy spoke. "Actually, John," she said, "I am going to leave you alone. For a while. I think daytime is a good time to leave you alone—can she come in the daytime? I don't think so. It seems to me that before she's only come at night. I'm going to go to the grocery store and stock up on some things." She rose. "I'll be back," she said.

At the top of the stairs, she turned. "John, I love you," she said.

But John was now asleep in his chair.

PUSHING HER RATTLING GREEN METAL CART DOWN THE AISLE OF THE A&P, Willy smiled idiotically. All this was so *normal*—these cans of instant coffee and baked beans, these plastic-sheathed loaves of bread. And the lucky, carefree people who shared the aisles with her, discussing the weather or last night's select-men's meeting—the sanity of it all was as exotic and tantalizing to her as a drug. She kept stopping her cart next to talking shoppers, pretending she was studying the labels of tuna fish, really eavesdropping on their conversations about weather and children and politics.

She was high; not happily high but alert, manic. She wanted to interrupt the two housewives with their lightship baskets over their arms, to touch them and say, "I'm going mad, I think. My husband's having an affair with a ghost, and I think I can do something about it. Don't you think that's mad?"

But she pushed her cart on by, automatically stocking up on food she could keep by her in the attic. Vaguely in the back of her mind were thoughts of siege.

She loaded the car with sacks of groceries, drove to the house on Orange Street, and then, on a whim, drove on past it, down Mulberry to Union Street, and back through town to Brant Point. She parked the car and, tying the hood of her parka tightly around her head, walked through the sand, against the wind, down to the edge of the water. Giant snowflakes fell on her, the air whirled with them; there were so many of them, and yet they fell in such complete silence.

This time the frosty air that bit into her lungs provided comfort. She breathed deeply, as if fortifying herself against the dark, cold claustrophobic air of the attic. Hands pushed down deep in her pockets, she stood on the water's edge and looked out at the sound.

Today had brought an Amsterdam sky, the kind that had taught Vermeer and Rembrandt about light. Fat blowing clouds, luminescent and pastel, low and laden with snow, their upper edges rimmed with golden light, hung over Nantucket Sound and the island. From these clouds the gentle snowflakes in their feathering fall whispered past great-masted fishing boats and the huge orange machines that were halted today from their work on the building of the new Steamship Authority building.

Willy turned slowly on the sand, not thinking now, just looking at the small boats rocking in the harbor, at the occasional parting of clouds so that a shaft of sunlight streamed down on the tall church tower while gentle snowflakes fell around it.

Her body was buffeted by icy winds. She let herself be hit and thought of how little she could imagine of life in nineteenth-century Nantucket. She had read *Moby Dick* and other accounts of whaling adventures, and now she remembered some of what she read: the disasters, the ships sunk in the black of night in the middle of the ocean, the limitless depths of the sea, the men eaten by whales or lost in lifeboats, starving, the women waiting on the lonely island, spending years and years without the touch of a man. Nantucket, Willy thought, is still one place where we can learn that this world is not the safe and tame place we would like to believe it is. So much is wild, so much unknowable—so much unthinkable. The world is as black and terrifying and cold as the ocean on a stormy night; as cold and heartless as her dream of falling helplessly through the icy void of space. There were mysteries and horrors and adventures and braveries that had happened in this world that were past her imaginings. Just thinking of this helped her now, gave her strength.

Flags of storm warning flew at the Coast Guard Station; by night this gentle snowstorm would be in full blast, and the sky would be as dark and raging as an ocean. The white snowy clouds, even now, were deepening, gathering layers and strength, turning gray. Only occasionally, as Willy stood watching, did the sun brighten the edge of the snow-heavy clouds. But when it did, those clouds became gilt-edged for a moment, and a path of sparkling brilliance fell through the air and across the land, and Willy knew that somehow there must be a love to save them all.

CHILLED TO THE BONE BUT SOMEHOW INVIGORATED, WILLY CLIMBED back into the Wagoneer and drove back into town. A thought occurred to her, and she stopped at the Atheneum and went in. The librarian, at her request, directed her to the Nantucket section in general and to the fat old tomes of Nantucket history in specific. Willy sat reading, feeling her fingers and toes tingling as they warmed up inside this graceful room. It was not long before she found the section about "The Widowed Bride," the same account that John had read. But Willy, although just as fascinated by the story and the pictures, did what John had not thought to do: She turned the page.

And found the rest of Jesse Orsa's story.

"Ha!" she said aloud, triumphant, bitter. And she returned the book to the librarian; now she was armed, ready to go home.

CHAPTER NINE

I T WAS JUST AFTER NOON WHEN WILLY RETURNED TO THE HOUSE on Orange Street. She dropped one load of groceries in the kitchen, then sprinted up the stairs to the attic to check on John. The sight and sound of the peaceful village and all the normal people who inhabited it, the housewives and checkers at the A&P, the librarian, the gum-chewing young girl who sold her her newspaper at the Hub today, had filled Willy with a sense of normalcy and optimism, and as Willy climbed the stairs, she said aloud to herself, "At least my heart will be in great condition after all this exercise."

John was asleep. He had moved from the chair to the bed and lay across it, uncovered, sunken in a profound sleep. He did not stir when Willy leaned over to brush his hair off his forehead.

Willy brought the comforter up and tucked it around him. She sat at his side on the bed awhile, looking at him. He truly looked horrible. And he had seemed physically weak today, shaking and debilitated. She could not remember when she had seen him really eat. But why would he be starving himself? It was just that he had seemed to lose all interest in food—and if he were having an affair with a ghost, or thought he was, no wonder he had lost interest in food. Loss of appetite was a common consequence of falling in love. Still, this was extreme, and she was worried. She determined that when he next awakened, she would make him eat if she had to force him at gunpoint. Although, of course, what a foolish thought; she didn't own a gun, didn't know how to use one. She would have to do something, though, to make sure he got some nourishment. If he wouldn't eat solids, she could make a rich, healthy eggnog.

Still he slept. Willy rose and walked around the attic. Aimee was curled up asleep in one of the brocade chairs. Willy ran her hand over the back of the chair; it was so lovely, so elegant, made of such beautiful material. Just now there was nothing in the attic that frightened her or that hinted of ghosts and passions and confusing jealousies. It was just a large, bright unfinished room with a marvelous view. Willy walked to the window and stood looking out. The clouds were darkening now, the snow was falling more thickly, and she understood that night would come early and with it a dangerous storm.

She spent the afternoon bringing in the groceries and preparing a small stockade of food for the attic. She brought a picnic basket filled with sandwiches and fruits, thermoses of hot coffee and tea, a flask of brandy for herself—just in case, she thought—a tin of cookies left over from Christmas. John still slept. After rummaging around in her sewing room, she chose several small pieces of embroidery work to do in the attic. She could not bring the banner of seasons for the church up; it was too large and needed to be spread out on a table. But she had a baby blanket she wanted to finish for little Peter and a summer nightgown she was decorating for herself. She brought up two novels and the newspapers.

Still John slept. She sat in a brocade chair, embroidering

while the afternoon faded away. She knew that if someone asked her now what she thought she was doing, she would have to answer that she didn't know, she wasn't even *thinking* about what she was doing. She was waiting. She was trying to be ready.

A little before five, she went down the stairs one more time. She had forgotten to bring up a tin of cat food for Aimee. She went to the front door, opened it wide, and just stood there awhile, letting the icy air blow over her. She stood there for the light, the remaining light, as if she could soak it in like a staying thing, as if she could stand there now and let the remaining light fall over her and close around her, providing her with a shield, a safeguard from the dark and whatever it might bring.

Orange Street was one of the main thoroughfares in Nantucket, a major one-way street running from the center of town to the airport and to roads leading to schools, residential sections, and shopping districts. Today it was strangely quiet, and no snowplows had come yet, so the street was sloppy with rutted snow. The wind was alive now, howling and whipping the snowflakes into frantic whirlwinds, and the heavy black cables enclosing telephone and electrical wires swung menacingly above the street.

The Constables had few neighbors now; most of the houses surrounding theirs were owned by people who lived elsewhere most of the year and opened their houses here only in the summer. So as Willy stood watching in the open doorway, she saw no warming glow in windows as people turned on lights in empty rooms, saw no familiar figures passing back and forth inside houses. The street was very quiet—except for the howling of the wind.

At last one person, so protected against the cold by winter garments that Willy could not tell if it was a man or woman, came past, head down, hurriedly stamping through the snow. Willy was so glad to see this real live person with its bulky hooded coat that she wanted to call out a greeting. But of course she did not. And soon the person was out of sight, leaving Willy feeling even lonelier than before. Night and the storm were closing in.

What shall I do, Willy wondered, shall I tie some garlic around my neck or tape two pieces of kindling together to form a cross? No, that's protection only against vampires, I think. She smiled at her thoughts, although she was shivering from the cold. Her teeth were chattering. But she was loath to close the front door and shut the house off from the rest of the world. When she did shut it, she did not draw the large brass bolt through as she did every other night. Tonight she was not afraid of anything human that might enter from the street.

The streetlights were on. The black night had come. Willy sighed and went up to the attic.

The door leading from the second-floor hall to the attic was shut and locked from the inside. Willy turned the handle, knocked on the door, pounded on the door, but it would not give.

She was shut out of the attic.

"John?" she called. "John? OPEN THE DOOR, JOHN!"

There was no answer. She pressed her ear against the door and listened. She could hear nothing.

"John!" she called again. "Dammit, John, come on, open the goddamned door!"

It was a heavy wooden door with an old-fashioned metal latch; the lock on the other side was a black metal bolt drawn through a metal ring. No key would open this door.

Willy raced through the house, turning on every electric light she could as she passed, and frantically searched through the cupboards in the kitchen for the household tools. But it was as she had feared: The tools were in the basement. Willy had always hated basements because of the odd mouse she had seen in basements as a child, because of old horror movies she had seen, and simply because she hated being underground in dank, shadowy places. She hesitated by the cellar door.

Then she unlocked it, opened it, and plunged downward.

The overhead light switched on by a hanging chain and swung eerily back and forth as she clattered down the wooden stairs. Shadows streaked back and forth around her as she moved. She and John had never been great as handymen, but they did own a tool chest, and she found it on an old table in the corner. She found the hammer. Nearly sobbing, she ran back up the stairs, leaving all the lights on.

"John!" she called when she was once again next to the attic door. "John, open this door or I'll break it down! I mean it! This is crazy! Open the door!"

She waited, listening, and then began slamming at the door with the hammer.

It was surprising how little effect her blows had. She might as well have been chipping at marble with a nail file. At first only the paint gave, cracking, then breaking away, but finally, after her determined hammering, the old wood began to splinter. She aimed her blows near the latch when she realized that she would not be able to break the entire door down, and after what seemed an eternity of frantic pounding, she had created a large enough jagged gap for her to reach her hand through the wood and draw back the metal bolt that unlocked the door.

As she drew her hand back through the wooden hole, the splintered wood rasped along her hand, cutting her, but she didn't care and hastily wiped the speckling streak of blood off on her sweater. She yanked the door open and raced up the stairs into the attic.

"Goddammit, John!" she called as she climbed the stairs, "what do you mean by locking me out, this is my house as much as yours, you have no right—"

But John was asleep on the bed. The heaters were off, and the room was painfully cold. The only light that was on was the one Willy had automatically pulled on as she came up the stairs.

"John?" Willy asked hesitantly. She crossed the room and looked down at him. He was profoundly asleep. The cat stood on the end of the bed, her fur ruffled, her eyes wide.

"All right, then!" Willy said, turning and addressing the air, "all right!" She stomped around the attic, exaggerating her movements, the force and noice of her actions making her feel braver and stronger and bigger. She switched on the heaters and turned on every electric light.

"All right," she said again, "go ahead and fight dirty. Fight as dirty as you can. I'll fight dirty, too!" She walked back to the bed, looking around her as she walked. "I'll tell John about you—all about you. I'll bet he doesn't know everything, I don't think he read everything, I don't think he turned the page, I don't think he knows the truth about you! Why, you're just pathetic!"

She knelt by her husband, and taking his shoulders in her hands, she shook him until at last he opened his eyes. It took him a few moments to focus, to see her, and then he said, so weakly she could scarcely hear him, "No, Willy."

"Yes!" Willy said. "You keep awake and you listen to me. John, I don't think you know everything about this gorgeous ghost of yours. I don't think you know that she needs you because she couldn't keep her own husband. He left her—" Still holding on to John, Willy looked up at the attic, where nothing was visible, but the air seemed prickling with a presence. "He left you, didn't he! Your husband left you for another woman! Ha!" Willy looked back down at John, whose head had fallen back and whose eyes were closed. "You listen to me!" she ordered. She propped him on pillows and rubbed and pulled at his face with her hands until he opened his eyes and looked at her.

"You didn't read the entire account, John," Willy said. "You didn't turn the page. It's true that when the Parliament returned, the officers told Jesse Orsa Wright that her husband had died at sea, but that wasn't the truth, and they all knew it. Gradually the truth filtered up from the crew to the town and finally to Jesse Orsa herself: Her husband didn't die at sea; he deserted the ship in order to stay on a Marquesan island, living with a brown-skinned, black-haired, illiterate island girl he had fallen in love with. He gave up command of his ship, he gave up his wealth, his entire way of civilized life, he gave up everything in order to live on an island with an island girl. *That's* why she wants you, John. She couldn't keep her own husband, and so she wants to steal mine.

"You're pathetic!" Willy shouted, enraged, turning back to whatever hovered in the air near her. "No wonder you're a ghost! If your husband had died at sea, your soul would be with his in death, but he was with another woman in life, and he's with her now in death. You're alone! You have no one, and so you want to steal *my* husband, and *I won't let you!* Ha, what a pitiful little thing you must be, you couldn't keep your own husband even after only a few months of marriage. Oh, John," Willy said, turning back to her husband, "don't you see?"

"It doesn't matter," John said, his voice a whisper. "That doesn't matter, Willy. I'm hers. It's done."

"No, it's not done!" Willy cried, but John's eyes closed again, and he slumped in her arms.

She let him fall back against the pillows, let the bed take his entire weight.

"Sleep, then," she said, "but I'm not leaving your side." Willy rose and clenched her fists and looked around her. "I'm not leaving him!" she yelled into the space of the attic. "You can't have him!"

The wind was screaming now, and shafts of icy air spun through the attic. With three small pings, the electric heaters went off and all the lights went out.

"It's all right," Willy said, talking to herself, to whomever, whatever, might be listening, "I'm not afraid. You can't frighten me. I can see from the window that the lights on Orange Street are out, too; they warned us when we moved here that the island often has power outages. I'm not afraid!"

Holding her sweater tightly around herself against the cold, Willy clattered down the two flights of stairs to the dining room, where she kept candles. She had many different lengths and colors of them, and she grabbed up a handful and two packets of matches and stuck them in her pocket. Then she lit a candle that stood in a silver candlestick on the dining room table, and walking carefully now so she would not create a breeze that could cause the flame to flicker, she made her way more slowly back up to the attic. She was shaking all over, and she was so alert with each one of her senses that she was in a kind of vivid pain.

As she walked down the hall from the first-floor staircase to the second, she glanced at the doorway to her sewing room. Even though the room was plunged into total blackness, Willy could sense that something was different there, and shielding her candle with her hand, she entered a little ways into the room.

The sewing room was in a shambles. Yarns and needles and material and threads lay in twisted piles on the tables and chair and floor. Unwittingly making whimpering sounds, Willy stretched out her hand and carefully drew into the heart of the room, trying not to step on any of the fabric.

Her banner of seasons was half on the floor, half on the table. It had been ripped into shreds and tatters. Willy turned slowly, looking around her, the candle throwing eerie shadows on the walls. Everything she had done in this room had been destroyed.

"Oh, God," Willy cried. "Oh, no." For now she had no doubts about the existence of the ghost. And now she feared its power.

She hurriedly left the room, once again shielding the candle with her hand. She climbed the attic stairs, feeling her heart swell with terror as she went farther up into the ghostly cold domain. Tears ran down her face, and she carelessly wiped away at them with the back of her hand.

Aimee was still at the foot of John's bed, making small

growling noises in her throat. Willy crossed the attic and sank down on to the bed at her husband's side. She could see by the candlelight that he was still sleeping. She touched his forehead. It was very cold.

"You wretched, pitiful bitch," Willy said aloud. "You can't have him."

I will sit here all night, she thought, I will sit here in the dark, I will sit here without leaving his side again, I will sit here if all the candles blow out, burn out, I'll listen to the wind howl, but I will not leave his side, I will not leave him to her.

But then she did leave his side, for just a moment, to fetch the flask of brandy from the table. She sat down next to John then and sipped the brandy, which burned her pleasantly. The cat moved next to her and settled down against her, not sleeping, very alert.

So Willy began to wait. In her mind it was the dawn that would save them; in her thoughts she had only to wait until the light came. She thought that as long as she was at John's side, the ghost could not come to him, could not take him.

But after a while a new fear came to her, a terrifying new thought, and she cursed herself for her stupidity, for her dull-wittedness.

The ghost was taking him now. How could she not have guessed? The ghost was taking him now, even as Willy sat by his side.

How incredibly stupid she had been, Willy thought. John was not sleeping. He was dying.

Willy took his hands in hers and sat there a moment, just holding her husband's hands, which were so cold. This is a poisonous trade the ghost is making, Willy thought; she is taking my husband and leaving me with her burden of grief and jealousy and bitter despair.

"Oh, God, help me!" Willy called aloud.

She threw back the covers and lay down next to her

husband, pulling his body against hers. He lolled next to her, as limp as a doll. She chafed at his hands and arms and face, trying to rub warmth into them. She put her head on his chest. His heart was still beating; it was racing. But his body was chilling, and his breath was shallow, and now she could not get him to come awake.

For one long moment, Willy felt the injury of defeat, which was colder than the negative air of the moon, which was more painful than the deepest cut. She thought of how her life would be if John died now, if he left her for the ghost of Jesse Orsa Wright. She knew that if this happened, the world would expand endlessly around her, an infinity of black despair.

As she lay on the chilling bed, holding her husband's body next to hers, Willy seemed to see, shimmering in the air beside her, the figure of a woman. It was not a clear figure, only a sense of outlined shining in the darkness of the attic, only a shape that was curved and bent in a posture of deep grief.

And Willy thought now, not of herself or of her husband, but of Jesse Orsa Wright, who had lived in this house a century ago, who had given up all chance of an elegant Bostonian life to come live on this isolated island, because she loved Captain John Wright above all other things. Willy thought of how it must have been for Jesse Orsa after she heard of her husband's death and then of his desertion—how that proud young woman would have lived her life in an agony of loneliness and longing and anger and grief, laughed at or pitied by the people of the town, who knew her husband had not loved her enough to stay with her, mocked by her own body, which craved the touch of the man she loved. Year after year Jesse Orsa Wright had lived this way, yearning to be held and touched and loved and admired, wondering what she had done or not done to cause her husband to desert her for an unclean, uncivilized native girl, grieving over all she had lost, all she had never had. And why did not Jesse Orsa Wright deserve to be loved and touched and admired and held? Why should she suffer so all through her life, through more than sixty years of life, and then through all eternity?

"My God," Willy cried, rising up on the bed so that she was kneeling next to her husband. "My God," she cried, and raised her arms through the dark, icy air of the attic so that she knelt with uplifted arms, supplicating any god that might be in the heavens or anywhere in the universe. "Dear God, if there is any goodness in you or in your world, there must be a love which will console this woman, which will soothe her, which will overcome her sorrow. Oh, God, there must be a love in this universe that is equal to this woman's grief! Or how will we all be freed from it?"

Willy seemed to hear her own voice echo in her ears. She heard nothing else except the wind tearing and pounding at the attic roof and windows and walls. It had seemed to her that she had truly seen a shape, shimmering through her tears, of a grieving woman, but now that illusion had vanished, and Willy knelt alone. The air around her was frigid. And she understood that she should not depend on God.

She had set the candlestick on the floor, and still the candle burned, its flame throwing off a small but definite light. Willy moved to the side of the bed and pulled her husband to the side so that she could see his face in the light of the candle. She pulled at him, she pulled up his eyelid; his eye was rolled up in his head. She could not wake him.

So now her grief and compassion disappeared, to be replaced with a singeing fear. Prayers would not save her husband now. At least not prayers alone.

Taking the candle with her, she went as hurriedly as she could through the dark down the stairs to the bedroom to call an ambulance. But the telephone was dead. Willy held the instrument in her hand for one long moment, wondering if it was the storm that had caused this or the ghost. In any case, she would get no help from outside this house, not unless she went out now and searched through the streets for a house with lights on and knocked on the doors and convinced some stranger to come back to this house with her.

She turned and went back to the attic. John lay collapsed as she had left him. The cat prowled, yowling softly, up and down the bed, all her hair ruffled.

Willy set the candle on the floor. She took her husband's arms in her hands and pulled on him. He did not come awake. She continued to pull at him, grunting slightly with her efforts. He rolled toward her at last, and as she knelt to take his weight in her arms, he slumped against her, sending them both sprawling onto the floor, knocking the candlestick over. The flame was extinguished. Her ankle turned under her painfully.

"Damn you, Johnny, help me," Willy said, trying to push her husband's helpless body off hers. He was as heavy and useless as if he were dead.

"Damn you, damn you," Willy said, crying now, fighting to get him off her so she could stand, and at last she was out from under him. She was sweating now in spite of the cold of the attic, and her hair had come loose from its braid so that it drifted across her face and caught against her nose, tickling her irritatingly. Somewhere near her in the dark, the cat mewed.

Willy bent over her husband and pulled at him. She managed to get him into her arms in a clumsy mock-lover's embrace that nearly broke her back. By bending over nearly to the floor, she could keep her arms wrapped around him just under his arms, so that his head lolled and his legs dragged backward. In this way she began to maneuver across the attic toward the stairs.

It was when she was at the top of the stairs, catching her breath before attempting the descent with him in her arms, that she felt the resistance. He was not resisting. Her husband was limp in her arms. But now when she pulled, it seemed that he weighed a thousand pounds. Her greatest effort could not seem to budge him. He weighed more than a piano, more than a house. Straining, gasping, Willy pulled on her husband's body and knew the ghost was using all her invisible powers to hold him back.

Willy sat down on the top step and rested there a moment, panting. Aimee was nervously rubbing against her, making questioning mewing noises. Now that Willy's eyes had had time to adjust to the total darkness of the attic, she could see how the windows were just a faint bit brighter than anything else; how they seemed like squares of exploding radiance. It was the blowing snow. The wind caused the falling snowflakes to burst against the windows in random spatters, and for one long moment Willy was mezmerized, watching. Then the wind gained force again and battered the house, howling as it hit, making the house creak and groan with the impact.

Willy could make out certain shapes in the attic now: the bed, the chairs and tables, and the looming, large canvases, so dark that she could not make out what was painted on them. She could see the dark shape of her husband's body where she had dropped him next to her. She took a deep breath. She willed herself to be strong and brave and sensible. She took his arms with her hands and pulled with all her might.

She could not budge him. It was not that he didn't move but, rather, that, as she pulled, a force stronger than hers resisted, pulling John in the opposite direction.

"Shit," Willy said under her breath. She was as angry as she was frightened.

She moved around behind John then and instead of pulling began to push. He was almost over the top of the first stair, and she hoped that once she got him going, gravity would come to her aid. Kneeling next to him, she placed her hands on his back, and with all her strength, she pushed. Grunting with exertion, she pushed. Aimee mewed next to her. Willy took deep breaths, trying to calm herself, for she was sobbing with frustration and with effort. The wind hit the house with a roar, and Willy shoved her husband's body one more time with all her might. Slowly his body moved to the edge of the step, so that his head thumped down onto the top step, and then she got his upper torso over, so that gravity did take hold, and John began to slide with a rough, uncontrolled thumping, down the stairs.

Willy hurried down alongside him, trying to catch him now in his fall so that he would not hit so hard. She managed to grasp his head in her arms, and they both tumbled, pushed by the impetus of his fall, to the bottom of the steps. They landed, sprawled and bruised and battered, against the broken attic door.

It was not over yet. Willy could tell that. She rose to her feet and pushed open the attic door, but now each movement she made took all her willpower and strength. It was as if she were trying to move her limbs while they were encased in cement. It was an awkward, weird, silent battle she found herself waging, a clumsy, stumbling fight. She felt like a creature caught in a straitjacket.

But she had just as much manic, insane, fierce, desperate strength. Now she lost all civilized restraints, and her grunts turned into deep animal groans that tore from her stomach as she fought to move herself and her husband into the hallway of the second floor. Her tears had stopped; she had no energy for crying. Her breath came in pants. She was not afraid or even thinking; she only pulled her husband, then squatted, resting, catching her breath, then grabbed hold of him and pulled again.

In this way she maneuvered herself and her husband to the top of the staircase leading down to the first floor. At the bottom of the first floor stood safety, Willy thought: the front door. She would open the front door and get them both out of the house. She did not think the ghost had jurisdiction outside this house.

She did not want John to make his way to the first floor in

the same manner he had gotten down from the attic—not that dangerous headfirst free-falling sprawl. She was aching from it and knew that she was bruised, contused in places. She could not see her husband clearly in this dark hall, but she was afraid the fall had battered him badly. He was still breathing, and his heart was chattering along in his chest, but he was very cold and showed no signs of consciousness. She did not want to endanger him any further.

The staircase to the first floor was longer than the one from the attic, the rise of the stairs higher. It was an elegant descent, but it could be treacherous, especially now that John was unconscious and Willy so weak.

She took a deep breath and summoned up all her energy. She hoped that the ghost's power would be weaker on this floor, this far from the attic. She was bending over to take John in an embrace when she first heard the cat's fierce cry—"Wrrrrrow!"—and then felt the stunning blow.

She was shoved by two hands with such force that she nearly flew through the air. She screamed, reached out to grab hold of something, anything, and crashed downward, falling against the banister. The weak balusters snapped immediately, and Willy fell through them, pitching downward like a person sucked through the teeth of a whale. Instinctively she clawed at the steps and caught a fingerhold in the carpet runner at the edge of the stairs. While her hands caught her, holding her arms and upper body firm, her legs and torso swung downward until she was lying against the stairway wall, swinging slightly.

She could not keep purchase here; so, not knowing in the dark how far she had fallen, how close to the first floor she might be, she let herself drop to the floor.

She landed with a painful crash; it felt more as if the hard surface of the floor had flown up to smack her than that she had fallen. The wind was knocked out of her. She lay still a moment, her whole body cramped in one long agonizing ache. At last, like a knife coming to her, her breath came back. Carefully she put her hands at her side and pushed herself up into a sitting position. She moved her legs and arms. Nothing was broken.

The hall was a well of darkness. Looking up, she saw how the darkness deepened toward the top. Up there lay her husband. Up there waited the ghost. Willy heard whimpering noises and realized she was the one making them; she clutched her arms to her chest and stood a moment just holding herself, trying to gather strength. She did not know if she had the courage, after that sickening fall, to climb to the top of the stairs again. But she had no choice. She could go out now in search of help, of course, but she didn't know where she would find it or how long it would take—and while she was gone, the ghost would have John alone to herself. It was not a risk she could take.

The cat mewed from the top of the stairs, a questioning mew that gave Willy courage. And then, for even more courage, she dragged herself to the front door and pulled it open.

The fierce winter night blew in. Like a madman in a rage, the wind slammed its way into the house, screeching its anger, pounding at the walls. The bitter cold shocked Willy. But the hallway filled with a slight bit of wavering, unsteady, snow-blown light.

She mounted the stairs. She hugged the wall, kept her back to the wall as she walked, and crouched as low as she could. She did not go all the way to the second floor but reached up with her arms and took hold of John's body so that his head thumped down and rested against her chest, and in this way she negotiated her way down the steps, bumping her husband's body down each stair but protecting his head with her own body.

She did not stop when they reached the first floor, but kept on moving so that she propelled them both out the front door and out of the house into the wild winter night. She stood on the front-door stoop, gasping like a woman nearly drowned, felt the snow slap against her, and began to cry with triumphant, exhausted sobs.

The lights were still off on Orange Street. From where she stood searching, she could see no signs of life or light. She knew John could not last long in these frigid temperatures—nor could she.

Her coat hung on an elaborate Victorian walnut hall tree just inside the front door. In her coat were her car keys, she was sure. If she could get her keys, she could drag John to the car and drive him to the hospital. All she had to do was to get her keys.

All she had to do was enter the house, a simple, everyday movement she had performed hundreds of times without thinking. It would take only a matter of seconds.

But for a moment she did not think she could force herself back through the doorway, which now seemed a portal to hell. Out here it was freezing, but inside it was as black as the tomb. Willy felt caught like a child in a nightmare, unable to move, unable to take the first step.

Then she realized that she could not seem to feel John's heart beating beneath her hands. She bent her head frantically over his face, shoving her hair away from her ear, trying to listen for the sound or feel the slightest movement of his breathing, but the churning snow made this impossible. Her hands were nearly numb with cold, but the fear that this was not the reason she could not feel his heart was what gave her the courage to reenter her house.

She was certain that as she entered, a wail as loud as a plane screaming above the earth broke out around her, but later she discovered that no one else heard such a noise that night. Still, it seemed to her that she had to move through sound in order to reach her coat and that that sound was a piercing, shattering shriek of grief. She drove herself through the sound

184

like a swimmer diving through dark waters. She tore her coat from the walnut coatrack and stumbled gracelessly from the front door. Terrified, she felt in the coat pockets: The familiar cold metal shape of the keys made her laugh out loud with relief.

The rest was easy. Or later she would remember it as being easy. She managed to drag her husband to the Jeep, to shove and force and bend his body into the vehicle. She climbed into the driver's seat and with shaking hands got the key into the ignition. After a heart-stopping moment, the cold battery roared to life, and miracle of miracles, the lights came on, great, powerful silver beams that caught the snowflakes in their dance.

She knew the way to the hospital. It was difficult on the snow-covered roads, but it was not long. She was sure the ghost was no longer with her, and so she was not so afraid. But she would not leave John alone while she went into the emergency room to get help; she parked the Jeep and dragged him in her arms to the door of the building. A nurse on duty inside saw her and hastened to let them in. The hospital blazed with lights and warmth created by the emergency generator. Willy smiled at the nurse before she passed out at the nurse's feet.

CHAPTER TEN

THEY KEPT JOHN IN THE HOSPITAL FOR THREE WEEKS. BECAUSE the diagnosis was severe malnutrition and nervous prostration, he was kept in a dark room, his body fed with a series of IVs. The first week he was comatose.

They kept Willy only overnight. She had so many scrapes on her arms and bumps and bruises on her head and body that they watched her for a brain concussion, and she had to be brought out of the state of shock she was in. But by the next morning she was in a good enough condition for the doctors to let her leave the hospital.

Because she had to tell them something, these kind doctors and nurses who had their forms to fill out, she told them that John was an artist. That she had been away for three weeks and she had returned to find that he had been working so hard that he had forgotten to eat sufficiently. That she found him in the attic in such a weakened state that it was necessary for her to drag him down the stairs herself and that the weakened balustrade had given way so that she had fallen from the second floor. And that was true, that was all true. It was also true that

186

she had tried to call an ambulance and found the phone dead because of the storm. There was nothing for them to doubt in her story.

When the cheerful nurse entered her room in the morning and whisked away the hospital tray that held Willy's breakfast and said happily, "Doctor says you can go home now!" Willy had felt something recoil inside her. *Home.* She did not want to go "home," not back to that house on Orange Street. She was afraid to go back.

But looking out the window, she saw that the day was sparkling with the aftermath of the storm. The snow-covered landscape seemed sprinkled with glitter, and the sky was a sunny, innocent blue. What bad could happen on a day like today? She would be fine.

Besides, she had to see about the cat. Poor Aimee; it was not much of a home Willy had brought her to. Willy wondered if the front door was still wide open.

So she signed the necessary forms, and after a brief glance at John's sleeping figure, she pulled on her coat and left the hospital.

She found the house filled with a crisp, gleaming, refreshing winter's light. Someone—no doubt some kind stranger passing by while walking to Main Street—had closed the front door. Willy stood just inside it, hand on the doorknob, ready for a quick escape. She could hear the furnace working away steadily in the basement; she could even feel the refrigerator thrumming in the kitchen. The life of the house seemed intact and pure.

But the splintered, cracked, and broken sticks of wood that had once been balusters lay scattered across the first floor, reminders of Willy's fall the night before. Willy looked up the staircase, where shards of wood still hung from the top railing. For one long moment she did not know if she would ever have the courage to climb those stairs again.

187

"Aimee?" she called, partly for the cat's sake, partly just to hear her own voice. "Aimee?" She was so worried that something had happened to the cat.

But Aimee came to the top of the stairs and looked down at Willy. She opened her mouth to mew, stretched as she did, and her mew came out in a comical yawn.

"Thank God!" Willy said.

Still she knew she could not spend another night in this house, especially alone. She summoned enough courage to get herself up to the second floor, where she hastily packed a bag. Then, without a backward glance at anything, she grabbed up Aimee and left the house.

FOR THE THREE WEEKS THAT JOHN WAS IN THE HOSPITAL, WILLY stayed in a guest house with the cat. On the first day, she called a real estate agent and put the Orange Street house up for sale. The agent told her not to expect a quick sale—it was the wrong time of year—but that when the warm weather came, she would easily find a buyer. Willy kept putting off a date to take the agent through the house.

That first week, Willy spent much of her time sitting by John's hospital bed, waiting for his return to consciousness. She had a great deal of time to think, although her thoughts seemed to go in circles, leading to no sensible conclusion. When she wasn't with John, she was taking her meals in the guest-house dining room or sleeping. She was very tired. She realized that she had a lot to recover from, physically and emotionally, and so she let herself rest. She lay curled late in the morning or early in the evening on the large antique four-poster bed in the guest house, Aimee snuggled next to her. She listened to the sounds of the house around her, the other guests coming and going up and down the stairs, the newlyweds laughing and nudging each other, the owner of the guest house walking through the large formal front parlors, arranging flowers, setting out fresh ash-trays. These sounds soothed her soul, and she lay immersed in them, as if in a certain safety.

For that first week she did not call Mark and Anne. Rather, she nursed a grudge within her and let that grudge grow. She hated them for not believing her, for deserting her, for letting her fight this fight alone. Mark had scoffed at her when she had called him for help. Anne had been too busy with her baby to even come to the phone. Willy thought she would never call them again.

By the end of the first week, John had regained conscious-ness. Still, he was weak. He opened his eyes, he spoke sensible words to Willy—simple words that he would have said to anyone: "Hello," "Thank you," "I feel better," "Okay." He did not ask Willy how he had gotten to the hospital. He did not reach out for her hand or tell her that he loved her. But at least he did not call out Jesse Orsa's name.

One week after her fall, Willy sat watching John, who lay staring out the window. It had gotten dark; there was nothing there for him to see. Still he stared, his face aged and sad, and he did not seem to realize, or to care, that Willy was in the room. Willy began to cry softly. She turned her head so John would not see. When she looked back, his eyes were closed, and he was asleep.

That night she called Mark and Anne when she got back to the guest house. She needed to hear the voices of friends. She determined not to tell them anything, not to let need show in her voice; she would only ask them how they were, if they were over the flu, how the baby was.

"Willy!" Mark shouted when he answered the phone. "My God, where have you been? We've been out of our minds worrying about you! We've called your house a dozen times and no one's answered. What's going on? Are you okay? How's John?"

The concern, the friendship, the love in Mark's voice,

made Willy's throat swell up, and she could not speak for a moment. When she finally did manage to talk, she heard herself, through tears, begging Mark to come to Nantucket. Mark said he would come.

~~~~~~~~

IT WAS EARLY EVENING. WILLY HAD JUST LEFT THE HOSPITAL. JOHN LAY still in his white bed, his thoughts filled with shadows. He was not satisfied. A faint, tantalizing, thrilling music flickered just at the edge of his consciousness; he knew it was Jesse Orsa calling his name.

It was easier than he had thought it would be to remove the tubes stuck into his arms. He knew his clothes were in the closet; he pulled his trousers on, tucking the hospital gown inside. He dragged his sweater on over his head, pulled on his socks and shoes.

No one saw him leave the hospital. He walked out of his room, down the hall, down the stairs and out the door without anyone stopping him, without anyone calling out or questioning. It was as easy as falling through air.

The evening was mild. There was no wind. John walked fast and did not feel the cold. In a matter of minutes he was on Pleasant Street, and then on the narrow one-way street that led between houses and gardens to wide Orange Street, where his house stood.

He knew the front door would be unlocked, and it was. Inside, the house was warm and quiet. He could tell immediately that Willy was not here. He could hear Jesse Orsa singing and laughing, teasingly calling his name. He climbed the stairs with ease.

The attic was illuminated by the street lamps; he did not need any other light. He saw the candlestick and candle lying on the floor by the bed and thought nothing of them. He saw his paintings leaning against the attic walls; those he thought of, for a moment, with regret.

He thought of Jesse Orsa, of her perfect body, her luxurious, seductive, greedy love. He did not let himself think of Willy.

Jesse Orsa was calling him. Her voice was like a song, the sweetest song. He had to strain his ears to hear. She was what did not exist on earth; she was a mirage, a reflection on water, a trick of light. She was all that was not real, and yet she would be real to him. If he reached out, he could be the person who held light in his hands, who could see music before his eyes. With her he could do all this; he had done it with her before.

So he climbed the slanted wooden steps to the widow's walk. Carefully he unlatched the hook the carpenter had attached and lifted the glass door upward and back. The cold night air flowed in around him.

John climbed out onto the widow's walk. He stood for just a moment, looking out over the rooftops of Nantucket. He saw far below him the glistening waters of the harbor and the gleaming church spires. Dimly he heard the gentle buzz of noise of this little village. He heard Jesse Orsa call his name.

With ease, with grace, with one swift, simple, exhilarating movement, he flung himself from the widow's walk into the welcoming spacious air.

JOHN LAY SAFELY IN HIS HOSPITAL BED, AND HIS MIND RANGED FREE. Perhaps it was simply that his body, in its fierce, independent acceptance of the nourishment flowing from the IV and of the true rest he was receiving now, was, in its one-tracked, unimaginative, unimpeded, completely physical way, rejoicing at his return to health. And so he was on a physical high that was causing the vividness of his vision. Perhaps that was so.

But this vision was as real as anything else in his life.

John saw himself stepping off the widow's walk into the dark void and knew that this act held the same kind of bravery and curiosity as those actions of the educated sailors and their illiterate crew who sailed their ships away from the safety of land into the vast, terrible seas.

He thought of the men who lived on whaling ships for years, touching no women, hearing no civilized songs, feeling the ever-changing turbulence of the ocean as it sucked and slammed against the ship instead of the steadiness of land. Seeing the blackest nights and brightest days men could see. Feeling extremes of heat and cold and hunger and thirst and fear and triumph and awe. Those men had committed sacred acts, as did any mere human who ventured forth into the unknown.

John saw himself stepping off the roof of the house on Orange Street, and it was as if he were setting forth on a voyage. He felt himself fall, the dark air surging upward past him, like waves sweeping past the keel of a ship, chilling him, purifying him, transforming him. He saw his body land hard and break and felt his spirit immediately rise—a miracle, it was like flames shooting upward from the heart of the sea. And he knew that who and what a person was was always a fiery thing, no matter the vessel that contained it.

He saw Jesse Orsa waiting for him in the darkness. He felt the flames of his spirit spiral around a center, and looking down, he saw that he possessed his body once again; he saw his hands, his feet, his arms, shimmering into shape. Why did people think that ghosts were cold?

He saw Jesse Orsa smile and hold out her hand. She was very lovely, as lovely as he had ever seen her, the sweet pink skin of her body showing through the lace and satin gown she wore. Her dark hair was piled in an elaborate fashion, adorned with jewels. He knew that she was dressed in celebration of his arrival.

The known world had vanished. John knew only darkness and the presence of Jesse Orsa and the fire that both consumed and provided him. A sound like kettle drums or deep thunder throbbed around him.

Slowly, John realized two things: that if he went with Jesse Orsa, he would never be with Willy again.

And he would never be an artist of any kind.

What was Willy to him?

She was his wife. She was the pattern of his days, the rhythm of his years, the orange-and-brown leaves of autumn that dipped in the breeze, the heat of summer, the food and hearth that warmed against the winter's chill. She was the woman who had chosen him long ago and stayed with him through eight years of changes and angers and compromises and perplexities. She was his friend. Her love was a lover's love, and more, because she saw him truly, not as an illusion, but as he was. So her love was the love of an equal, and she needed him and required of him all the things she gave.

In some way she was part of him even now; she was there, flame in flame that burned in him, inseparable.

She needed him, she wanted him, she called him back. Even though Willy was not present in the hospital, seated next to him, calling his name, still John heard her call him, through the flames, for Willy and John were husband and wife, and her needs burned through him—her voice, her incandescence as smooth and brilliant as a mirror, reflecting his own gleaming heat.

This was their marriage. It was not every marriage. Jesse Orsa had not had that with Captain John Wright.

John saw Jesse Orsa waiting for him. He knew she saw him in his body, handsome and young and willing. He sensed how she saw him, how in spite of her own ghostliness she could not see the fire burning in him.

He saw that because Jesse Orsa was a spirit lost in longing, she wanted of him not who he was in all his depths and complexities but who he was simply, superficially: his body, as it was now, because it resembled her husband's.

But Willy wanted all of him, greedy spirit and cantankerous mind along with body, the real body, that was now young and handsome but that would eventually age. Willy would love him as he grew old; as he would love her. It was Willy who wanted him, and so he wanted Willy, who loved and accepted him, surface and depths.

In his vision, he chose Willy.

And with Willy came the knowledge that he could try to be an artist. Perhaps only that, only *try*. If he left the living world now, *he* would know secrets. But he could never pass them on. If he lived, he could try to explain what he had learned. He could try to portray light held in the hands, music seen with the eyes. There were no guarantees that he would succeed.

But for him, the voyage, the curiosity, the attempt, the bravery, lay on earth, not here in death.

The challenge of his life would be to paint, to paint what he had learned here.

Jesse Orsa held out her hands, and there was a question in her eyes: Why was he delaying?

John shook his head.

"I am so sorry," he said. "I cannot come with you."

"But you *can*!" she called.

"I won't," he replied. "I want to live."

Her eyes blazed with anger. It seemed her body shimmered and sparked. He felt her flare with rage and indignation. Even so, she was very beautiful. John knew that somewhere along the years she would find a man who pleased her who would not be able to resist her many lures.

In spite of her brilliant anger, John saw Jesse Orsa fade. Or perhaps it was he who was fading. The darkness they were in was being invaded by light, and the fire within him steadied so that the outline of his hands and arms became clearer. He was returning to his hospital bed. He was returning to what he had chosen: life, and Willy.

He fell into a deep and healing sleep.

THE FOUR FRIENDS SAT IN THE HUNTERS' LIVING ROOM IN CAMBRIDGE; they were laughing and drinking champagne. Aimee lay curled on a sofa cushion next to Willy. Baby Peter lay on a blanket on the floor in the middle of the room, staring enraptured at the light bouncing off the silver champagne bucket. From time to time he cooed at it and reached out to touch it; feeling the cold, he shrieked. Anne had out her address book; she was writing names, addresses, and telephone numbers down for John and Willy. "I don't care about everyone else, but you've got to call the Martins," she said. "They're more fun than anyone in the world."

"We may not have time to see anyone," Willy said, "if John gets involved with his painting."

"I'll make time," John said. "I promise. I'm not going to let two months in Bermuda go by without some sunshine and good times."

"I think I'll get pregnant," Willy announced, stretching her toes out to warm them by the fire. She laughed all by herself at the others' expressions. "Why not?" she asked.

John grinned. "I'll see what I can do for you, lady," he said.

"Oh, you're so lucky!" Anne exclaimed. "Two months of sunshine and sex by the sea!"

"You should write ad copy," John told her.

"You *are* lucky," Anne said. "You know you are."

"I know," Willy agreed, leaning toward John.

"I know," John said, pulling his wife close to him. "God, do I know."

The four sat in silence, sipping their champagne, watching

the baby kick and gurgle on the floor. They heard the fire crackle and tasted the bite of alcohol against their tongue. They were happy.

When Mark had come to Nantucket a few weeks before, summoned by Willy's call, he had quickly taken charge. He had escorted the real estate dealer through the house because Willy didn't have the heart to do it; he had cleaned up her sewing room first. And he had carefully packaged up all of John's finished canvases and taken them back to the mainland with him. While John lay recovering in the hospital, unaware, Mark, with Willy's permission, took the paintings to various galleries in Boston.

No gallery liked the black paintings, but several had expressed interest in the nature studies: the shell and feather, the few harbor scenes. One of the better galleries had taken some paintings on consignment, and a painting of feather, shell, and berry had already sold. It brought only a few hundred dollars, but it had sold.

John was elated. He and Willy had already decided that they needed to go away somewhere for a while, to get far away from Nantucket and winter and all that had happened so recently. The owner of the gallery had advised him to paint more water scenes, more nature scenes; John was good at that, the owner said, he would like to see more. So John and Willy were going to Bermuda for two months, to work and lie in the warming sun, to be together. The cat would live at the Hunters' while they were gone. When they returned, they would look for a new house in Boston.

John had never been happier in his life. He liked to think that he would have been this happy without having had a painting sold, but that was not true. To have his work validated in this way meant a great deal. Meant he was beginning, could begin. And this was almost everything.

But not quite everything. He was an artist, he knew that

now, and because he had had a painting sold, he could do the work he wanted and feel right in his actions.

But he was also a man, one who had had an unusual experience—and now in this glow of health and happiness he knew he could not swear, if he had to, that that experience had not been an imaginary one. The important thing was what he had learned from it.

What he had learned was not easily called forth. Now that he was sensible and sane, on his feet again, *normal,* he knew that he had had a vision, but he could recall it only vaguely. Some days it flared up in him so that he could almost articulate it, almost express it in words. But then it would vanish, leaving him with a powerful desire, like a thirst or a sexual ache—and then he would paint.

Now and then bits and pieces of the vision would float up into his consciousness, emerging like a fish flashing up from the sea or the gleaming, bizarre flipping of some sea creature's fin, throwing off light, causing an eagerness, a hope. Then it would disappear. Then John would paint.

Someday, he thought, he might catch it, all that he had seen and experienced and learned, someday, if he kept at it, if he dedicated himself and worked hard. Perhaps he might never catch it with words, might never be able to say to other people: This is it, this is what I know. But he might paint it. And that challenge lay before him; the meaning of his life.

The challenge was now the meaning of his life, and Willy was, as she had always been even when he did not know it, the vital necessity.

Willy was his harbor, his anchor—his safety net.

As he was hers.

It was possible that there would never again be with Willy that searing flash of lust and fear and awe that came with first love. Perhaps that could only come with what was new and strange and unknown—and unknowable. Or perhaps not—

there had been times both before and after the ghost when John knew physical love with Willy that was so powerful it frightened him.

But it was probably true that there would never again be that terrifying fall from the luminous, lucid world into the dirty, dangerous, carnal dark. He could have chosen that, but that was not what he wanted.

What he wanted, rather, was life, life with Willy. With Willy he could try to remember it all, the voyage, the stepping into dark air; he could take the voyage, he could step into dark air with his art—and if he failed, fell, Willy's love would catch him. And if he succeeded, for he would often succeed, Willy's love was still there, the way that clouds wait beside a plane. The way a marriage waits while the man and wife sleep through the night. The way the sun waits for the earth to turn toward the light.

And there would be times, he knew, when Willy would need his love as a safety net. And he would be there for her.

Perhaps when she started her embroidery work again. Perhaps when she got pregnant. Perhaps even as soon as tonight when they made love.

For sometimes when they made love, Willy would cry out with ecstasy and fear, she would cry, "Oh, John, I'm so high!" And John would hold Willy and soothe her and love her and bring her down safely in his arms.

AFTERWORD

A STREET IN NANTUCKET . . ." IS NOW CALLED HAWTHORN LANE, from the jungle of twisted hawthorn trees that line it on both sides, the most gnarled, thorny hawthorn trees that ever defied the approach of man.

"The legend is that they are the reincarnation—if one may use that word—of all the unhappy old maids who lost their loves at sea, or had their lovers taken from them by girls at other ports, or never had any lovers at all, and lived long, thorny, gnarled lives ever after. Once a year, in May, they bloom a virginal white. Once a year, in October, their branches are hung with red berries like drops of blood from a deep wound. And all the year they stretch forth their savage thorns."

William O. Stevens, *The Faraway Island*
(New York: Dodd, Mead & Company, Inc., 1936)